ONE HUNDRED LESSONS

AN ASPEN COVE SMALL TOWN ROMANCE

KELLY COLLINS

BOOK NOOK PRESS

CHAPTER ONE

Mercy Meyer wasn't looking for Prince Charming. At thirty-five, she'd kissed one too many toads to know he didn't exist. The idiot she married had warts and all and look where that got her.

Three piles of bills sat on her table. There were those she couldn't pay, those she would pay—eventually, and the companies who could kiss her behind.

The largest stack was from the first pile. She chipped at them little by little, but each one she sent money to, only opened the wound of her husband's betrayal more. It was a good thing he was dead because if she knew then what she did now, she would consider murder a viable alternative to the pain she suffered.

The squeak of the chair, grinding against the hardwood, made her teeth clench.

"How does an insurance salesman have the worst policy ever?" Randy once told her that life with him would always be interesting. She picked up the tallest pile of mail, at least twenty envelopes deep, and tossed them across the kitchen.

Marriage was supposed to be a partnership where two people worked together for common goals. These days, she worked to avoid late charges and hits to her credit score.

"What a Wonderful World" by Louis Armstrong filled the air, and she picked up her phone. Did Mom have a sixth sense and know when she was down in the pits of despair?

"Hey, Mom."

"Good morning, Mimi," her mother said. The nickname came from the first two letters of her full name. Mercy Meyer—me and me, but when you put the two together, you didn't get Mimi but meme, which had a whole different meaning. She tried to explain it to her mom one day, but Milly Meyer lived by her own set of rules.

"How are you, Mama?"

"Can't complain. Daddy got me up early." She giggled, and Mercy knew exactly what her parents were up to that morning.

"You two give me hope."

How long had it been for her? She couldn't remember the last time she enjoyed herself between the sheets. Although Randy had the perfect name for sexual shenanigans, he was far from perfect at giving her lady bits a thrill.

Between his "late nights" and "conferences" and "consultations," he didn't have room in his schedule to make love to his wife because he was doing it with everyone else. Where had she gone wrong?

If she learned one thing during the whole debacle, it was she couldn't trust her judgment when it came to men. For her, it was a game of straws, and she managed to choose the short one each time.

She pulled her bucket list from the kitchen drawer and added earth-shattering O to the next blank line on the page. That came after finding a good man and becoming a mother. Her priorities were definitely askew. Should the big O really come after finding a man and becoming a mother? She drew an arrow to tuck it between the entries.

"Are you still there, Mimi?"

"Yes, sorry. I dropped some mail." She bent over and gathered what she tossed across the floor.

"Well, I want you to know, you deserve a good man too."

"You know any?" It wasn't that she was opposed to trying her hand at love again. She cast her line into the pond a few times, but men were always looking for something different. She was a salmon egg when they were looking for a worm or power bait.

"What happened to that bookstore owner? I thought you were setting your sights on him." Mama might be getting on in years, but she never forgets a thing.

Being the youngest of five, Mercy was an oops baby but loved as if she were the first. What her parents had was what she wanted—deep connection, passion, and a family to call her own.

"He found the love of his life in the diner. Natalie is a sweet girl and deserves something good too."

"Oh, honey, you deserve a man who appreciates you for who you are and what you offer."

"My prince will come." She wished she truly believed that.

"No, baby, don't wait for him to come. You need to get out there and find him yourself. Just set your standards high."

She turned the page of her notebook. "Okay, Mama, what should be on the top of the list?" She took a seat and readied her pen.

"Single."

Mercy swallowed the lump in her throat because single didn't mean faithful.

"Okay, single and devoted. Who knew an insurance salesman could have groupies?" Randy wasn't a rock star, but there were several women at his funeral that Mercy didn't know, and their tears were too many for a casual acquaintance.

"Did I tell you about the time I was a groupie?"

It was hard to believe her mom was anything other than a housewife and mother of the year. "Is this the Kenny Loggins story or the Dan Fogelberg tale?"

"Both. The point is, maybe you should try being a groupie once. It's very freeing."

Mercy flipped the page back to her bucket list and put groupie on the top.

"There is a band living in town." With Samantha's band in Aspen Cove to record a new album, there were options, but she wasn't looking for temporary. She wanted a forever man.

"That's the spirit."

"Nowadays, there's more to being a groupie than following the band for a summer."

Her mother laughed out loud. It was a sound that brought back memories of game nights and firepits and s'mores.

"Oh, there was back then too. Nothing wrong with having a summer of love before settling down."

Mercy was done settling in her life. She settled for a lot of stuff, including a small wedding, a used car, and an apartment when she wanted a house. However, the last time she settled turned out to be a blessing in disguise because she would have been saddled with a mortgage payment if she hadn't.

"I still remember making love all night long on every surface in the room. I swear that's how I ended up with that slipped disc in my back," her mother said.

"Geez, now I have to wash my eyes out with soap and water to get rid of that vision of you and Kenny I conjured." Now that she thought about it, her older brother, Mike, kind of looked like Kenny Loggins. "Is Michael really Dad's?"

"Oh, honey, you know better than that. I didn't have Michael until Daddy and I were married over two years. Besides, your father wouldn't let me go to a concert alone once he learned of my wild ways, but as soon as your daddy entered my life, there wasn't anyone else I wanted. I mean, Elvis was dead, and Burt Reynolds was taken."

Why didn't I get Mama's luck and her zeal for life?

An exciting weekend was canning jam or going to Bishop's Brewhouse for a single light beer.

"Dream big, sweetie. Life never gives you exactly what you want, but it never hands you more than you can handle."

She didn't dare dream bigger. At one time, she wanted three kids by the time she was thirty. That ship sailed five years ago, and now her eggs were probably withered and dead, or those that were viable knew it was unlikely they'd ever get fertilized and exited her fallopian tubes on a waterslide to freedom each month.

"Daddy was a smart man to swoop you up and make you his." If he hadn't, her brother Michael might look like Burt.

"I tell him that all the time. Anyway, I called to make sure you were okay."

It had been a year ago today that Randy died in that car accident. At first, she was in shock, but as things unraveled, she experienced more pain than she ever expected.

"I'm okay. You don't have to worry about me."

"Oh, honey, you're my baby, and I'll always worry." She growled into the phone. "If that man hadn't had his pecker bitten off during the car accident, I would have severed it myself with that Ginsu your father bought me last Christmas."

The amazing Ginsu would do it. Sometimes life dealt us ugly hands, and sometimes it meted out justice. For Randy, a road blowie wasn't the smartest thing to do on a winding highway in the Rockies. At least he died on a happy ending.

"You know, Mom, the worst part was the humiliation. My life was a page right out of the National Enquirer." It was an article in that rag mag called *When Biting Off More Than You Can Chew is Deadly*.

Who knew her entire school district would read it? Their snickers and giggles were poison darts aimed at her soul. It was bad enough her husband cheated on her with a client, but it was the city councilman's wife, and that made the story newsworthy—infamous actually.

"I'm glad you moved away from there. Silver Springs was never the place for you. Are you still loving Aspen Cove?"

"Yes, I love it here. Too bad there isn't a school in town. The commute to Copper Creek isn't fun in the winter, but the school district is great, and the people are nice." She lucked into the job when the first-grade teacher at Creek Elementary got married and moved out of state.

"Are you sure you're okay?"

"I'm perfect, Mom, really. It's not like I'm mourning the loss. All is good." She was grieving, not the loss of Randy, but the loss of her hopes and dreams.

"Do you need money? I know they don't pay teachers enough."

"You're right, they don't, but I'm okay." She never let her family know the truth of it. Randy's insurance barely covered his burial. There were the charges for hotel rooms and fancy dinners he'd put on their joint credit cards. She still owed money on his car, even though it was totaled—once again because of a lack of insurance. Thankfully, she negotiated a lower payoff. Yep, he was right. Life with him and without him was interesting. "I love you so much, Mama, and wish you were here." Her parents lived in Arizona, where the weather was hot and dry and suitable for their arthritic bones. "Talk to you soon?"

"You know you will. Now go out and live a little."

"Yep, groupie is at the top of my list."

She hung up and laughed at the silliness of their conversation. What mother told her daughter to be a groupie? Apparently, hers did. She stared at the list. "Why not?" She'd seen Indigo play on the Fourth of July. The bass player was cute, and so was the guitarist. The drummer was a fan favorite, but not her type. She liked the clean-cut, not so gritty men. Besides, she couldn't fall for a man whose hair was prettier than hers.

In the living room, her basket of folded clothes sat abandoned, so she grabbed a pair of pink underwear she recently bought from Walmart and shoved them into her pocket.

There were three new houses built in Aspen Cove. Rumor had it they belonged to members of the band. She knew Axel lived on Rose Lane because Sosie, Baxter, and she had a conversation about tucking underwear into his chain-link fence, and while she said she'd never do it, she would today. Axel, or Alex, his real name, was the least likely to be a problem for her. He was so far from her type, which made him the perfect musician to test out her groupie skills.

Hopefully, those things were passed down the gene pool because she had no idea what she'd do if she got caught.

Dressed in jeans and a T-shirt, she walked out the door and prowled toward the drummer's house. Could she actually pass for a groupie in her Keds and Life is Good T-shirt?

The thought made her laugh so hard she snorted. She was a schoolteacher, and bagging a band member was only on her list because her mother told her to try it.

The extent of her efforts would be to shove her underwear in his fence and call it a day.

SHE LOVED summer in the mountains with the birds singing and flowers blooming. The weather was perfect, with a slight breeze that carried the scent of pine on it. As she neared Axel's house, her heart raced.

"You're not robbing the man," she said under her breath as she skulked up and down the block twice before gaining enough courage to approach.

She spent a moment staring at his house. Though

she wasn't up on styles, the word Craftsman came to mind. Though it was new, it blended in with the surrounding older homes. The only thing off was the fence. A white picket would have had more charm.

Sighing, she shoved the material inside a link and turned to walk away.

Just as she did, a truck turned the corner and drove past her.

She'd been caught and needed to save herself, or she'd be known as the pink panty prowler, and one scandal was enough for a lifetime. Tugging the underwear free, she moved down the sidewalk, pulling the other pairs from between the links.

Of all people to catch her, it was Baxter and Sosie. He rolled down his window and asked, "Everything okay?"

What could she say? She stared at her hand. How many had been worn? "Disgusting." Her gut response gave her an idea. "Can you believe women leave their underwear on the fence?" She held her hand out like she did a used Kleenex during flu season. "There are children in this neighborhood." She stomped forward, opened the neighbor's trash can, and tossed them all inside. "Somebody has to be the voice of reason."

"Carry on," Baxter said and drove forward.

Mercy couldn't see coming all this way to fail, so as soon as the coast was clear, she fished her panties from the trash can and tucked them into the fence before she ran off.

Her blood pumped so fast she thought she'd pass out. She couldn't call herself a groupie per se but had done a groupie thing and was now part of a crowd that left personal items as a sign of adoration.

"Oh my God, I'm like a cat who left a mouse on its owner's doorstep." She sped up and jogged toward her street.

When she walked into her house, she went straight to her bucket list and lined through the word groupie. Her walk on the wild side was over, and all it cost her was one pair of panties and self-respect.

She texted her mom.

Checked off groupie from my bucket list.

She watched the three dots scroll across the screen.

You are your mother's daughter and quick too.

If only she were as bold as her mother, she might not have settled for less.

I didn't sleep with anyone, just put a pair of underwear in his fence.

The dots scrolled again.

You're not supposed to put them in his fence; you're supposed to leave them in his room. Do I have to come there and teach you?

What a conversation to have.

Nope. I'm in training. You can't expect me to play the guitar if I've never had a lesson.

Dots and more dots.

Oh, is he a guitarist? They have nice fingers ... skilled fingers.

He's a drummer, and I don't want to hear about his rhythm or his sticks.

Scrolling ...

What about his wood? :-)

Bye, Mom

She tossed the phone into the drawer and walked into the living room where their last family photo sat on the mantel. Leaning in to look more closely at her brother, she realized he had Kenny Loggins' eyes.

CHAPTER TWO

Waiting for everyone to show up, Alex Cruz sat behind his drums and watched the video from the security cameras he recently installed. He promised himself he wouldn't be caught off guard the next time a fan decided to surprise him. He couldn't count the number of times he'd found a naked woman or two in his bed. That was the thing about groupies; they didn't mind sharing.

In Los Angeles, all it took was a hundred bucks to the right security guard, and they were inside.

He couldn't fault them. From the outside, his life looked glamorous, and all they wanted was a piece of the action. It was like they had a bucket list, and sleeping with him was at the top of it.

If he wasn't in town and managed to get into his

place, they stole the craziest shit like his soap or his magazines. He'd finally given up wearing underwear because his boxers disappeared faster than a coin from a magician's hand.

He played the footage of a blonde woman, placing a pair of underwear in his fence and then moments later yanking all the pairs left since yesterday and tossing them into the neighbor's trash can. A moment later, she took a single pair out and put them back in the fence.

"Ready?" Samantha asked, drawing his attention from his phone.

Red and Gray picked up their instruments. Deanna, Sam's assistant and all-around savior for the band, walked in with coffee and muffins, smiling at everyone but Red. He got a glare, and Alex wondered what was going on there.

"Let's do it," he said. While his voice sounded exuberant, his brain wasn't fully awake due to the earlier than ordinary session.

Samantha stood in front of the group. "I'm still working on getting a keyboardist." When she suggested they all move to Aspen Cove, Matt said no. He was a surfer through and through and wasn't living where there wasn't a beach with gnarly waves.

Deanna passed Alex a coffee. He didn't function until his third cup was down, but this would put enough zip in his veins to move his hands.

"What about a session player?" There were more musicians in the world than gigs. Once upon a time, he was a rent a drummer and played with anyone willing to give him a check. That was before Samantha found him filling in for the drummer of Rebel Riot, who opened her act years ago.

"I put out some feelers." From her bag, she pulled out sheets of music and handed them to everybody. "How is everyone settling in?"

"All settled and loving the place," Red said. "Thanks for the bonus."

"Yeah," Gray chimed in. "Loving my place, too."

She turned Alex's way. "You doing okay?"

"House is great." He held up his phone. "Still have a fence problem."

Samantha cocked her head to the side. "Did you call the Coopers?"

"Not that kind of problem." He set his coffee and phone down and pulled his hair back into a ponytail. It was his signature look, but it drew attention, especially in a town where entertainers weren't known to live. "Someone outed our location. That damn crazy 'superfan' posted my address, and now I have an underwear problem."

Gray's laughter rumbled through the room. "If you didn't have a chain-link fence, you wouldn't have a problem."

"If I didn't have a fence, I'd have a bigger problem. Just this morning, my cameras caught a woman leaving a gift. Thankfully, she didn't strip down to take them off right there."

Samantha shook her head. "That's just wrong. Not only is it a public nuisance, but hygienically, it's just gross."

Years ago, he would have disagreed, but now it was a source of irritation.

"Why chain link?" Samantha asked. "I think a wood fence or a block wall would serve you better."

He let out a whistle that changed tone with the shake of his head. "Could you imagine not being able to see what I faced. I can visualize it now. I'd enter the locked gate and get swarmed by naked bodies."

Red choked on his coffee. "And you call that a problem? With the lack of women in Aspen Cove, you should feel blessed." He turned to Gray. "Looks like we can hunt at Alex's place since the pickin's in town are slim." A blueberry muffin took flight from Deanna's hand and nailed Red in the side of the head.

"What the hell?" he brushed the crumbs from his hair.

"Sorry, thought you'd like a muffin."

He wiped a smashed blueberry from his temple. Something was going on between them.

"Do you kids want to talk it out, or should we get started?" Samantha asked

Deanna headed for the door. "I've got furniture coming, so I'll be gone for the day. I just wanted to bring you a snack and wish you guys luck."

"I don't need luck; all I need is sleep," Alex said. "I can't seem to hit REM until morning."

Samantha adjusted the mic. "What you need is a good woman who would give you a reason to come to bed early or tire you out so that sleep comes easily."

Deanna glared over her shoulder at Red and stomped out.

"What the hell is going on there?" Samantha asked.

Red's face turned the color of his name. "Too much wine and several poor choices."

"You didn't." Samantha scowled at him. "You understand I can replace you easier than her, right?"

Red scrubbed his face with his hand. "Look, we're both adults. Something happened, but we realized it wasn't smart to mix work and play. It will be all right."

"See," Alex said. "Women are trouble. I need a woman about as much as I need a concussion."

"I don't know how I work with you Neanderthals. Don't forget, without a good woman, you would have never come about."

That statement was both true and false. Alex wouldn't have come about without a womb, but the "good" part was debatable. What mother had a kid and then drank herself to death?

He picked up his sticks and started his standard warm up while the rest of the band got ready.

"Sound guy will be here in two hours. I think we can lay down tracks." Sam said. "If we hit it hard over the next few weeks, we can finish this album early, and you guys can take the rest of the summer off once we do the concert for the fire department fundraiser."

Red set the sheet music on the stand. "Something new?"

She nodded. "Yep, it just came to me. I'm calling it, 'Right Woman, Wrong Time.'"

"Story of my life," Gray said.

They played for several hours before the sound technician arrived. He wasn't their regular guy, but he was talented and efficient.

They gave Sam's new song a try, and it reminded him of his family. The apple didn't fall far from the tree. He was his father, from the sticks in his hands to the ice covering his heart. If he'd written the song, it would have been called, "Right Woman, No Time."

When Dad was alive, he played for the greats like the Stones and Skynyrd until he got a permanent gig with Drive Shaft. Tragically, he went down in a plane like so many do who travel from show to show. Worse was he was the only member of his band on that plane since he was hitching a ride with another group. Last year Drive Shaft got inducted into the hall of fame without him.

The lyrics were hauntingly familiar.

She needed more.

I gave less.

When it ended, I had nothing left to give, and she had nothing left.

It could have been written about his parents. His mom was a backup singer for a band. While they toured together, things were great. Then she got pregnant, and he left her behind to raise his son while he continued his life of debauchery. With Mom at home, she drank away her loneliness. For Dad, there was too much time and too many women. Dad was an asshole.

They went over the song three times before they called it a day, and on their way out, Gray tossed him a baseball cap. "Tuck that long shit up inside, and no one will recognize you. Without the hair, you look like a dad ready to coach a little league team."

Alex stared at the cap in his hand. Could it be that simple? Was a new identity all he needed? He tossed the hat back. "What if I cut it all off?"

Samantha dropped her mic. "No way. You've been sporting prettier hair than me for years."

It was true. He had better hair than most women,

but he didn't ruin it with curling irons and hair dye. He was a wash-and-wear guy.

He couldn't remember a time when his hair didn't hang to the middle of his back. It came part and parcel with his badass drummer image, but he was thirty-eight. Maybe it was time to let it go.

"Dude, I dare you to lob that shit off."

"But the ladies like it," Alex said.

Samantha walked up and yanked his hair tie out. "Yep, the same ladies who stalk you and leave you gifts."

Gray shook his head. "Don't do it. Changes like that could keep you celibate for years."

"Talking from experience?" Alex asked.

"Nope, I do fine with the ladies."

"I'm out," Samantha waved her hand in the air. "Hearing you talk about your conquests makes me want to write a song called, 'Men are Dicks.'"

Red raised his hand. "Guilty."

"I know." She pointed at him. "Fix whatever you have to with Deanna. I was serious when I said it would be easier to replace you than her." Samantha walked out the door.

Gray slapped Red on the back. "You're expendable."

Red looked around the studio. "We all are. Anyone want to join me for a beer?"

Alex shook his head. "Naw, I think I am going to get my hair cut."

Twenty minutes later, he was sitting in Cove Cuts, getting his gorgeous mane clipped by the sheriff's wife.

"Are you sure you want to cut it all off?"

He stared in the mirror at his long dark hair. It was time for a change, and if in the process it kept the crazies from pursuing him, then that was a bonus.

"Let's do it."

"You want to donate it to Locks of Love?"

"Sure, it would be nice to know someone benefits."

Hopefully, I will too.

She pulled his hair into a ponytail and chopped it off above the rubber band. She held up close to two feet of hair.

Immediately he felt much lighter and swore he was dizzy, or maybe that was the shock of seeing it all gone.

Marina spent the next thirty minutes shaping it up and giving him a haircut that would make a lawyer proud. When she was finished, he hardly recognized himself.

"I feel naked."

She laughed. "Trust me, you're not. But I think your hair looks nice. You can really see your eyes now and your chiseled jaw."

"Chiseled jaw, huh." If he didn't know she was madly in love with Sheriff Cooper, he would think she was flirting, but she wasn't. She was telling it like it was. He did have noticeable facial features now that his hair wasn't the focus. He rubbed his hand across his jaw. "Leave the scruff or shave it clean?"

"You can't take all the bad boy out of you."

He paid her and walked outside to give his new look a test drive. If the people who knew him didn't recognize him on sight, his fans wouldn't either. At least not until a new picture made the rounds.

He walked into Bishop's Brewhouse and sat at the bar.

Cannon approached and put a coaster in front of him. "Welcome to Bishop's, what can I get you?"

Alex looked straight at Cannon and ordered an IPA. Cannon turned to pull the beer from the tap and glanced Alex's way twice before his jaw dropped.

"Holy shit, I didn't recognize you."

Alex threw his fist in the air. "Mission accomplished."

CHAPTER THREE

Some of the bills Mercy had flung across the room yesterday still littered the floor this morning. While her coffee brewed, she ambled around and picked them up. Stacking them on the table month to month wasn't helping.

She glanced at the one in her hand. Theresa Taft Diamonds. That was for her wedding ring. She tried to take it back, but they didn't accept returns after a year, so she sold it for half of its worth. Actually, half of what he paid, which was far too much for what it was—a small diamond on a gold band.

She grabbed her coffee, took a seat, and closed her eyes. The memory of the proposal was still fresh. Randy was charming, and the courtship a whirlwind. In hindsight, she should have known he was capable of cheating. He picked her up in his office when she came for an insurance quote. He wasn't rich, but he was funny.

On the day he proposed, they went to the lake, and he got down on a knee. It was all so romantic.

"How did everything go to hell?" she mumbled.

The first year was great, and they had fun getting to know each other. He didn't make much money, so she was the primary breadwinner in the family, but that wasn't a problem because they were a team until they weren't.

After their first anniversary, he started complaining about their lack of money. That's when he began his habit of working late. When he smelled of perfume, she didn't worry because he was in close quarters with clients—clients who got more than insurance from her handsome husband. After the funeral, she found out Randy was a serial cheater. He liked the idea of being married to a pretty schoolteacher. It brought him a sense of respectability even though he wasn't respectful to her, their marriage, or his clientele. If he hadn't died, would she still be oblivious to his betrayal?

Slamming her palms on the table in frustration, she caused her coffee cup to spill over the edge. The bills soaked up the liquid in the same way they did every dime she made. How did a man with so little income have so much damn credit?

She had two choices: bankruptcy or another source of income. Randy stole her heart, her trust, and her dreams, and there was no way she was sacrificing her credit score too. She needed a second job; maybe someplace she could pull a few hours year-round to help make ends meet.

Determined to create a better life for herself, she dressed, put a little makeup on, and climbed into her car, an old Volkswagen Beetle decorated with flower stickers and peace signs. She wasn't a hippie, but she loved the happy-looking vehicle, and the kids at school got a laugh from it too. Each year the flower-shaped stickers seemed to reproduce. She was almost sure the glue on the backs kept her car together.

She pulled into the open spot in front of B's Bakery and went inside. If anyone knew about potential jobs, it was Katie. She had her ear to the ground in the small town. With the only bulletin board in town, she was privy to what people wanted and needed, and right now, Mercy needed money.

"Hey, you." Katie leaned against the glass display with a smile as sweet as her brownies on her face. "What brings you in?"

Mercy didn't indulge in baked sweets often. First, they weren't in the budget, and second, they were like a drug to her. Once she started, she wouldn't be able to stop.

"I'd love a cup of coffee." She looked at the sweets behind the glass and sighed.

"Muffin?" Katie pulled out a cranberry orange treat and set it on a plate. "On the house."

"It's not that I can't afford it." She tilted her head to the side. "Things are tight, but a treat now and again is in the budget."

"Take it and have a seat. I made too many today—besides, it's your compensation for having to sit with me for a visit. With the town growing and all, everyone is busy, and my lady friends don't have as much time. If Sage isn't working, she is usually taking a nap, and Lydia never leaves the clinic unless she's with Wes. Louise has eight kids, so how much free time do you think she has?" Katie nodded toward the door. "Natalie used to come in every so often, but she's got Will and Jake, who keep her hopping." She got Mercy's coffee and jutted her chin toward the table. "I need my girl time."

"I could use some girl time too." Mercy felt terrible that she hadn't gone out of her way to forge any relationships in town. She knew of just about everyone but didn't actually *know* them. After the public scandal and all the tongue-wagging she had to deal with, she'd taken a people hiatus since she arrived. It was time to become part of her community.

They moved to the table under The Wishing Wall.

"Tell me, where have you been hiding?" Katie asked in her Texas twang.

Honesty was at the forefront of her prerequisites for human interaction. She didn't have it with her husband and wouldn't tolerate not having it with anyone else, but did she come out of the gate with her dilemma or ease into it?

"My life has been a bit of a challenge since I moved here." She leaned in and whispered. "My husband passed away last year."

Katie's smile fell, and a tear pooled in her eye. "Oh, honey," she reached over and took Mercy's hand. "I had no idea. I'm so sorry."

While the sympathy was sweet, it wasn't necessary. "Um ... thank you, but I have to be honest. Randy was a cheating, lying, sack of shit."

"Oh," Katie's eyes shot wide open. "Karma is a bitch, isn't it? If I caught Bowie cheating on me, I'd castrate him."

The death of Randy wasn't a laughing matter, but Mercy laughed loud and hard.

"Karma did that for me. Car accident."

"Seriously?" It took a few seconds, but Mercy knew when Katie figured it out. "Not that guy."

"Yep, he was mine ... well, not really. Apparently, he was a lot of peoples."

"Oh, you poor sweet thing." Katie leaped out of

her chair and wrapped Mercy in a hug. "Girl, you should have come in here earlier."

"It's so embarrassing." Her cheeks heated, and she was sure they resembled the color of a cranberry.

"That was his sin, not yours. His stupidity, not yours. His punishment, not yours." She hugged her tightly for a few more seconds before taking her seat.

"That's where you're wrong. I'm still being punished." She glanced at The Wishing Wall. "Do people ask for jobs up there?" She pointed to the corkboard.

"Oh lord, they ask for everything from bigger you-know-whats, to a cure for hemorrhoids. The stuff I see could make a person want to bleach their eyes."

"I thought I'd come in and put my wish on the board. I need a summer job for now and a part-time one once school starts. Do you know anyone hiring?"

"Dang it. I wish you'd come and seen me yesterday. Samantha's crew is in town, and since there isn't much nightlife here, Deanna picked up a part-time job at the bookstore. I don't think she needs it for money, but to ease the boredom of living in the sticks." Katie stared out the window. "With that walking around town, I don't know how any girl could get bored."

Mercy turned around to see what grabbed Katie's attention. Across the street was a man walking into the pharmacy. He was tall with short, dark hair.

Though he looked vaguely familiar, she couldn't place him.

"Who's that?"

"Only the biggest heartthrob to move into Aspen Cove. It's Alex Cruz."

Mercy pulled a muscle snapping her head to look where the handsome man entered.

"No way. Alex has long flowing brown hair. That's definitely not him."

Her fingers crossing her heart, Katie said, "I'm telling you. He ditched the Rapunzel locks—had Marina chop them off yesterday and donated them to that place that makes wigs for cancer patients."

"Aww." She softened at that. Any man who donated his hair to help someone feel better was okay in her book. "That was so sweet."

"Not sure if he did it because he was sweet or tired of the stalking. The poor man has so many groupies he can't get a moment's peace. Women stick their underwear in his fence."

Could a heart beat right out of a chest? Was this Katie's way of telling her she knew about the pink panty caper? Nothing in her eyes said she was aware that Mercy shoved hers in his fence.

Mercy's eyes rolled skyward. "Oh yeah, most men would hate skinny, willing hotties hovering. It must be awful having women throw their lingerie at him and offer sex on demand."

"You're probably right. I imagine he has a line at his front door while he escorts the flavor of the day out the back. He's probably in Doc's stocking up on protection."

"Do you think he gets a discount for ordering in bulk?" She imagined a room in his house delegated to groupies. One wall was stocked floor to ceiling with condoms, and the only other thing in the room was a bed.

"Don't tell Bowie because he's the only man for me, but if I was single ... I'd stand in line. I mean, can you imagine the skills he must have? They say practice makes perfect."

"That kind of practice keeps doctors busy prescribing antibiotics." She couldn't believe she said that out loud.

She and Katie looked at each other and busted out in laughter. "I like you, Mercy. I wish I could offer you a job, but Ben takes all the hours here." She glanced across the street. "Rumor has it that Phillip and Marge are selling the Corner Store, but there aren't jobs there until there's a new owner."

"They're leaving town?"

"It's not public knowledge, but they're getting on in years, and the store is a full-time job for both of them. I heard they were buying an RV and traveling." She reached up and took a pen and a sticky note from the basket hanging on the wall. "Fill out your wish, and let's see what happens. This town is a place of miracles."

The door opened, and Alex looked behind him like he was being followed, but no one entered.

Mercy tucked her head down and wrote.

I need a job ... any job.

Mercy

Katie stood behind the counter and gave Alex her big-as-Texas smile while he ordered several muffins, cookies, and brownies.

From beneath her lashes, Mercy chanced a few glances his way. This couldn't be the drummer from the band. He went straight from the cover of Rolling Stone to GQ. She would have thought the haircut would make him look older, but it didn't. He looked more refined and less bad boy, but the smile he gave Katie as he paid said his haircut didn't tame him.

When he turned to walk away, she tucked her head down.

"Holy hell," Katie said after he left. "He's hotter now. I love a good man bun, but those eyes could hypnotize a girl, and that smile even made my ovaries do a double flip, and I'm married to the hottest guy in town. No wonder women throw themselves at Alex."

Mercy took a five from her purse and set it on the counter. "It was good to get some time to chat finally. Let's do coffee again." Despite the black cloud continually hovering overhead, Katie was a ray of sunshine. Everyone needed sunshine in their lives.

Katie pushed the money back toward her. "His smile was payment enough. It makes me feel like giving everything away for the day."

Mercy went back to the table and tacked her wish to the wall. "He's okay, not really my type."

"Oh, honey, don't lie to yourself, Alex Cruz is everybody's type."

CHAPTER FOUR

"Three more pairs of underwear and a cake with, 'Call Me,' written across the white frosting, were in my fence or by my fence this morning."

Gray chuckled. "I had a naked girl on my hammock asking me to be her baby daddy, but when I walked out the back door and she saw it was me and not you, she said I'd do in a pinch but wanted your address to see if she could upgrade."

"You're kidding."

"No shit, man. These women are crazy for you. The only good thing is, now that the stalkers have arrived, there are more women in Aspen Cove."

Was it true that there were only a few single women between the ages of legal and dead? If so, that had to be a blessing because women were nothing but trouble.

"The bad news is we might get chased out of town by the residents who aren't used to, let's call them *music enthusiasts.*"

"The deputy sheriff didn't seem to mind when I called this morning and had him pick her up. Dude's name is Merrick, and he's as big as a house. He didn't intimidate the woman, though. She offered to get warmed up with him."

"He can have her and her ticking clock lady parts. I'm not going to be anyone's baby daddy. I've avoided parenthood up to now, and I'm not going to screw it up with a one-night stand." Alex's outer voice always managed to keep the inner one in check. There had been times when he saw a child playing and felt the tug of want, but "the apple didn't fall far from the tree" was a saying for a reason.

His father wasn't ever around, and his mother was a drunk. There was no love between them because he never changed his lifestyle when he got her pregnant. He'd done the right thing and married her, but that only gave her hope he would come home and be a husband. Dad was married to the music, and Mom to a dream.

They finished laying down the track Gray wanted to re-record and went their ways.

His stomach growled. Yep, just like his dad,

putting music first and forgetting about everything else, including food.

He hopped in his car, a brand-new navy-blue SUV, and drove straight to Maisey's who could silence the tummy grumbling quickly with her blue-plate special.

When he walked inside, he scanned the nearby tables. He spotted a blonde who didn't look like his usual type of follower with her makeup-free face and ponytail. Her look screamed librarian with her floral skirt and sensible shoes.

Intrigued, he moved in her direction, and the closer he got, the more familiar she became. She was the pink panty girl—the one who couldn't decide if she wanted to leave them or take them.

Engrossed in a book, she didn't notice his arrival until he slid onto the bench across from her.

Her eyes snapped up and opened wide, the look on her face was shocked. He didn't know her, but by the recognition in her expression, she knew exactly who he was.

"If you're missing your pink panties, I found them."

She opened, then closed, and then opened her mouth again.

"Who are you?"

He leaned over the table. "Take a closer look darlin', you know exactly who I am." Then he pushed back until his spine flattened against the back of the booth. "What do you get out of leaving your underwear on my fence? I have to say, you don't look like the type."

She took three breaths and appeared to grow with each one. "You mean, a big-boobed, botoxed bimbo?"

Seemingly affronted by his accusation, he wasn't sure if her agitation came from getting caught or being categorized as one of many.

"See, you do know me."

"Hardly. And I don't know what you're talking about. My underwear is on my person, and the only time I take them off is for laundering."

"You don't know what you're missing." Initially, he intended to shame her for her behavior, but now he was egging it on.

She crossed her arms over her chest with a huff. "Would that be gonorrhea?"

"Never had it. Never will. Safety first and fun later." He slid from her booth. "You are a young, attractive woman, and you should be having more fun." He turned and walked away. *Shit, that whole exchange sounded like a pickup when it was the opposite.*

He moved several booths away and sat so that he faced her. With her long blonde hair and sweet country smile, she wasn't his usual devotee. He attracted women who were a tad higher maintenance. Her description wasn't too far off.

Maisey moved toward him at lightning speed. She didn't have to look where she went because she walked through the restaurant like it was a memorized maze. She said, with her eyes on her order pad, "What's it going to be." She glanced up. "Holy hell, what happened to your hair?"

"I imagine it's on its way to some woman who needs a wig." That made cutting it off worth it.

She stared at him for several seconds, then smiled. "I like it. It suits you."

He raked his hand through it. It would take a lot of getting used to, but it was easier. All he had to do was shower and add some hair gel, and he was set. His longer hair took hours to dry.

"What do your friends think?"

"They think I look like a little league coach."

"Honey, if there was a little league coach who looked like you when Dalton was growing up, I would have been the team mother." She tapped her pad. "Blue-plate special?"

"Yep, that's how I roll. I'd love a glass of water too."

She scribbled his order on the pad and took off with her white loafers squeaking with every step.

He stared at Blondie in the booth. He hadn't noticed the crayons on the table or stacks of cardstock.

She was entirely focused on her project and not him. Maybe he was wrong about her being the one who left her pink underwear. If she were a fan, she wouldn't ignore him. Instead, he'd be calling Merrick to get her removed from his booth.

A few minutes later, Maisey delivered his plate of chicken-fried steak, mashed potatoes, and green beans smothered in butter. He lifted a bite to his mouth and caught the blonde woman looking, but she immediately lowered her head.

A blush rose from her neck to her ears—cute ears with a single pearl in each rather than the big O hoops. Deanna's voice came into his head, *The bigger the O, the bigger the ho.* Now that would be a song to write.

He did his best to ignore her, but each time he glanced her way, he found her looking back. It wasn't with adoration, but something that looked like confusion.

The bell above the door rang, and he turned to see a woman and a small child enter. The woman in her thirties glanced his way and marched toward him.

She looked familiar, and so did the kid, but he couldn't place either. She stopped in front of his table and stared.

"You won't remember me, but maybe you'll remember her." She yanked a picture of a dark-haired beauty from her purse. "You and Layla hooked up in Madison while you were on tour."

The woman in the picture had eyes the color of robin's eggs and a mouth that ... yep, he remembered her. She also had a drug problem. After their second night together, he found her in the bathroom with lines of the white stuff.

She showed up at several of his concerts after Madison, but he had her escorted out. He didn't do drugs, never had, and never would.

She tugged the little girl forward, so she stood in front of him. Her eyes weren't like her mother's, but a combination of green and blue.

His heart stopped beating long enough for his head to spin. Her eyes were just like his.

"Why are you here?" He prayed the little girl was hers, and they were passing through, but he knew better. She entered the diner on the hunt, looking for him, the prey.

"This is Madison, and she's yours."

His world tumbled off its axis. "How do you know?" The words came out without thought.

"Because she said so." She pointed at the picture. "Layla was a lot of things, but she was never a liar."

The woman opened her bag, which was large enough to hide a body. She pulled things out as Mary Poppins did. First was a manila folder, next was a small photo album. He looked at the little girl again.

Really seeing her this time, he noticed the small teddy bear she hugged to her chest and the tiny wheeled suitcase sitting next to her—things he hadn't seen when they arrived.

"What do you want? Where is Layla?" He had so many questions. His eyes drifted to the blonde in the booth, who'd taken a keen interest in what was happening.

"Her mother is dead." She leaned in and whispered. "Drug overdose."

That didn't surprise him. "Again, what do you want?" He imagined this was an extortion attempt.

"Nothing. I'm doing what I told Layla I would do if anything ever happened." She looked at Madison. "She left behind directions, if you know what I mean."

Holy hell, she killed herself. This was his worst nightmare—life repeating itself. "Why?"

"She was a mess."

"Because of me?" His throat tightened.

"Drugs, depression, and a diagnosis of breast cancer," she said. "No insurance, no money, no hope."

"Was any of this my fault?" he always felt responsible for his mother's death. She died the first year he went on tour. He was another man who had let her down.

"Don't be so arrogant. You were a blip on her radar. If she hadn't found that fan's site which listed your digs, Madison would have gone into the system, but now she'll go with you."

"What? I can't..." He stared at the little girl who bit her lip and looked ready to burst into tears. "I'm not ready to be a dad."

"No one is." She opened the folder. "Here's her birth certificate. You're listed as the father, so there are no custody issues. Layla left you a letter." She touched the photo album. "I gathered the pictures I found. It would be nice if you could help her remember her mom."

"You're leaving her with me?"

"Yep, I've four kids of my own, and my mother won't watch them forever." She laid her hand on Madison's head. "She's smart but behind in her learning. Layla wasn't much into school, so she didn't have a lot to offer." She kneeled, so she was in front of Madison. "Hey, Maddie, girl, this is your daddy. He's going to take really good care of you."

Madison or Maddie started to whimper. "I want to go with you."

"Sorry, kid, we don't always get what we want." She kissed the top of her head and stood.

She turned and glared at him. "Don't be a shit to her. She's had a rough life already. Make it better." She spun to walk away.

"Wait. What's your name?"

"Doesn't matter." She walked out of the diner.

His heart raced while his stomach flipped. What the hell was he supposed to do? He didn't want a kid and had no idea what to do with one. The tiny whimper he heard seconds ago coming from Madison turned into a full-blown cry.

He had no nurturing skills. Absentee dads didn't raise sons who would become the father of the year.

"Madison, you need to stop crying."

The little brown-haired girl with his eyes looked at him and cried harder.

"Madison, please stop crying." He attempted to move out of the booth toward her, but she stepped back.

"I'm not going to hurt you." That was a damn lie. He'd never physically hurt her, but it was in his genes to fail at parenthood. That's why he never ventured into long-term relationships. His career of choice made it hard to establish trust.

"Maddie," he said, and she stopped the sounds even though her tears still fell. "Is that what you like to be called?"

She nodded.

He'd only heard her say a few words. The woman who brought her said she was behind in learning. He didn't even know how old she was.

"Have a seat, and we'll get to the bottom of this." He pointed to the bench across from him, but she didn't move to it. Instead, she turned her suitcase on its side and sat on it.

Maisey swung by. "Who's this little beauty?" She stared down at Maddie, who was in the middle of the path.

"Apparently, she's my daughter."

Maisey dropped her order pad. "Oh my. What are you going to do?"

What was there to do? As far as he knew, the kid could be anyone's. He wasn't the only man in the world with hazel eyes and brown hair.

"First, I'm going to read the letter her mother sent, and then I'm going to get proof."

Maisey leaned down to pick up her order pad. "You hungry?" she asked Maddie.

Maddie nodded. "I wike chicken."

"So, she talks. That's a plus."

Maisey scowled at him, then turned back to the child. "Nuggets and fries it is."

He opened the folder and found Maddie's birth certificate with him listed as the father. Madison Alexandra Cruz was born five years ago on June 10th. He pulled out his phone and scrolled back in his calendar. Nine months before June would have been September.

That feeling of falling raced through him. On September 18th, he was in Madison, Wisconsin.

Fear clawed past his belly and crawled into his

heart. There was a reasonable likelihood Maddie was his.

His fingers shook as he took the letter out of the envelope.

Axel,

I never asked you for anything until now. Take care of my baby.

Layla

"What the hell?" He looked down at Maddie, who clutched her teddy bear like it was the only thing she had left on earth, and by the looks of it, that might not be far from the truth.

CHAPTER FIVE

Mercy watched everything unfold. A rock star. A child. A dead mother. Her heart ached for the little girl. She considered how terrifying it must be to be shoved in front of a stranger and told, "he's your daddy."

As a first-grade teacher, her business was children. She loved them all—even the little heathens who stuck boogers under the desk. Children were programmed to mimic their parents. The thought of Alex Cruz being this child's role model made her cringe. He was an arrogant asshole, and that was the impression she got after a few minutes. How would she feel after an hour? Two? A day? A month? Perfect smiles, hot bodies, and full, no doubt, soft lips might satisfy a woman short term, but they weren't the qualities needed to raise a child—a child obviously traumatized by her mother's death.

Maddie's despair pulled her like a magnet to a fridge. She slid from the booth and inched toward her, so she didn't startle her.

"Hey, you?" Lowering to her haunches, she smiled. "How about we get you seated at the table? I bet your nuggets and fries are almost ready."

Maddie looked at her with eyes that could melt the heart of the hardest man, and Mercy hoped they would soften the hard expression on Alex's face.

She held out her hand, and Maddie stared at it warily.

"It's okay," Mercy said softly. "Everything is going to be okay." She knew when her students were troubled, all they needed was a hug and someone they could trust. "Do you need a hug?"

Maddie inhaled a shaky breath. She lifted from her seat on the Disney Princess suitcase and fell into Mercy's arms.

Holding Maddie made her realize how much Randy had stolen from her. She should have had her own child by now but would have to settle for loving everyone else's.

Mercy stood, holding Maddie and her bear in her arms. "I've got crayons at my table. Would you like to see them?"

She felt the nod against her chest. Hugging

Maddie close, she walked to her booth and sat her in the seat in front of her current project.

"Hey," Alex said. "What are you doing?"

"What you should have. I'm comforting her and redirecting her energy toward something positive."

He stood and looked at the cutouts she laminated each summer and used in her classroom.

"A fish is positive?"

"It is to a confused little girl."

She lined up several primary colors and spread a few of the fish in front of Maddie. "Do you think you can make these look pretty while I talk to him?" Mercy nodded her head toward Alex.

Maddie picked up the red crayon and started coloring. As soon as the sweet little thing was occupied, she walked to where Alex stood.

"Wow," he said. "How did you do that?"

"I have an empathy gene. Which is something you seem to lack."

He stared at her like she'd spoken a foreign language. "I can empathize. She's lost her mom, but what am I supposed to do about it? I mean ... what person leaves a kid with a stranger?" His voice hitched up a notch with every word.

"Someone fulfilling the wishes of a friend, I guess. It was misguided and not thought out, but somewhere in the craziness, I imagine she thought she was doing the right thing."

He peeked around her. "I can't keep a kid. Hell, I don't know if she's even mine. Just because someone says so doesn't make it true. Her mother was a groupie."

In a whispered yell, Mercy said, "That woman was her mother, and there's a good likelihood you could be her father. The last thing you want to do is make her feel unwanted."

Her head snapped around to look at Maddie, who moved the red crayon and drew hearts all over the next fish.

Feeling the heat of anger rise, she gave him her best teachers, do-what-I-say look, and pointed to Alex's booth. "Have a seat. You and I need to talk."

Like a star student, he did what she said. He lumbered to the bench and sat.

"Why do you care?" His hand ran through his short hair, leaving it sticking up like a kid who'd woken from a nap.

"Because I know what it feels like not to be wanted."

"Is that why you left your underwear in my fence? You wanted me to want you?"

She gripped the edge of the table until the blood left her fingers. "This isn't about me and whether I did or didn't leave my panties in your fence."

He grabbed his phone, moved his fingers over the screen, and then shoved it in front of her.

Her whole groupie experience was on security footage. She wanted to melt into the seat and disappear.

"What does that have to do with Maddie?"

"A lot. You're chastising me for my behavior when yours is questionable."

She couldn't argue with that. A part of her wanted to grab his phone and find some way to delete the recording. What would her peers think if they saw the video? Mortification sat like a brick in her gut.

She nodded. "You're right, and you can flog me later, but right now, you need a plan for Maddie. What are you going to do?"

He let out a grunt. "I'm going to call child services. I mean ... who abandons a kid in a small-town diner?"

"Are you kidding me?" she asked through gritted teeth. "What if she's yours?"

"What if she's not? Maybe this is some crazy way for a mother to get her daughter a better life."

Getting arrested for assault wouldn't be good for her career, but Mercy was ready to throw a punch. "You have a big ego. Too bad it's pressing on your brain, making it inactive." She let go of the table edge and flexed her hands to get blood flow to her numb fingertips. "In what world would living with you provide that beautiful little girl a better life? Money doesn't buy happiness."

His head moved side to side. "Nope, but it buys clothes, a better education, good food, and a roof over her head."

"If that's the case, then the mother failed. She considered you to be a decent man—a man who would look at that sad little face and feel something other than inconvenience."

"I don't have a clue about raising kids."

"You were one once. Just remember the good times and try to repeat them, and let the bad times be a lesson for what not to do. Child services should be your last resort. It's not that they're a bad organization. They do wonderful things for kids, but if you're her father, do you want to put her in a system where she'll most likely see several homes before her eighteenth birthday? Where she'll always wonder what was wrong with her for her parents not to want her?"

He groaned and scrubbed his face with his palms. "I never wanted kids."

She pushed herself against the back of the booth. The more inches she put between them, the safer Alex was. Generally, she wasn't a violent person, but she was a fierce protector when it came to children.

"If you didn't want kids, you should have made sure you were shooting blanks."

Alex's body twitched. "I always use protection."

"Nothing but sterility is a hundred percent. If you whip out the fun gun, you need to accept the responsibilities of firing it."

Looking like a ghost dripping sweat, Alex nodded. "I hate that you're right, but you are. Do you know where I can get a paternity test?"

Maisey dropped off the nuggets and fries to Maddie. "Sorry sweetie, Ben ran out of the frozen ones and made these especially for you. They're not nuggets, but chicken fingers."

The sweetest giggle came from Maddie. "Chickens don't have fingers."

Mercy looked over her shoulder to see Maddie's tears had dried, and a hint of a smile played at the corners of her lips.

"You're so smart," Maisey told her.

A full-blown smile appeared on Maddie's face showing a single missing tooth that made her look more adorable than ever.

Mercy leaned to the side so Alex could see. "That, right there, should be your goal every day. I imagine she's seen enough sorrow for a lifetime. Make her smile, Alex. A million childless people would want to be in your shoes right now." She was one of them.

"As for the paternity test ... see Doc. If he can't do one, then I'm sure he knows someone who can. Until you know, don't make decisions that you'll regret later."

"I've got a lot to think about."

Mercy inched toward the edge of the booth. "Don't think, do, but make sure it is the right thing." She got up and took a seat across from Maddie.

While the little one gobbled up her chicken and fries, Mercy said a silent prayer that she'd be all right. She glanced over her shoulder to where Alex sat stiffly. His face took on the green hue of a kid who ate something bad. She could let herself feel sorry for him, but what good would that do? Alex wasn't the one who was homeless and at the mercy of an adult who didn't want children.

That seemed the way of things. Those who wanted children couldn't have them. Those who did often didn't want them or couldn't provide for them.

What she wouldn't do for a man to show up and tell her a child was hers. It was a crazy, impossible scenario, but she'd be overjoyed. Hell, she'd even be thrilled to have a woman show up and tell her she had Randy's baby and hand the child over to her. It didn't matter whose body a child came from. What mattered was whose heart they'd live in.

On that thought, she gathered her things. "You keep the crayons and the fish. I've got to go, but Alex is right there, and he'll take care of you." She hoped she was right. "Hopefully, I'll see you soon." Before she packed up, she gathered her things and stood to leave. "Maisey is right. You are a smart girl." She bent over and kissed the top of Maddie's head. "Be brave."

She walked past Alex and said, "be kind."

"Wait a minute. What's your name?"

Mercy almost told him, but she remembered the video. "It doesn't matter. Do the right thing and be the best you."

"What if the best me is sitting here, right now?"

She rubbed her temples. "Learn to be better."

CHAPTER SIX

Alex moved from his booth to where Maddie sat coloring fish. "Did you get enough to eat?"

She nodded and went back to decorating the fish.

He watched her a few minutes. She was a lefty, just like him. Her hair was darker than his, but in the same range of brown. It was possible that it fell in the color range between his and her mother's.

She looked up from her coloring and cocked her head to the side.

Staring at each other, they were like adversaries analyzing the opponent.

Maddie slid a fish across the table. "Here."

He glanced at the fish and blue crayon she gave him. How long had it been since he colored anything? His childhood wasn't crayons and sandwiches with the crust cut off. It was holding Mom's hair when she threw up or checking on her in the middle of the night to make sure she didn't drown in her vomit.

"You want me to color one of your fish?"

She nodded.

He picked up the crayon and made stripes from lips to fins. What was he going to do about this little girl? He needed a plan and fast.

Maisey moved by. "Do you two need anything?"

His gut twisted. "More than anyone can provide at this point. I have no idea what I'm doing."

"Looks to me like you're coloring, and that's a start."

The crayon broke under his tight grip. "Can you tell me how to get ahold of the doctor in town?" What he needed more than anything was confirmation. There wasn't much sense in making plans if Maddie wasn't his.

"I can do better than tell you; I can introduce you." She stepped back and pointed to an older man sitting in the corner, reading a paper and sipping coffee. "That's Doc right there. He won't mind if you go over for a chat." She looked around the diner. "I'll sit with Ms. Maddie and color."

Alex moved out of the booth, and Maisey moved in.

Bothering the man on his break didn't seem right,

but desperate times and all that. He drifted toward the corner booth.

"Excuse me, sir. Are you the town doctor?"

"Parker," the man laid down his paper and held out his hand. "I'm Doc Parker, but everyone calls me Doc. What can I do for you, son?"

The way he called him son scratched at his insides like sandpaper. He was no one's child, especially not the two people who procreated him; he was more of a child of the world. His parents were merely a vessel and a paycheck. How he made it to adulthood was a surprise.

"I apologize for interrupting your solitude, but I have a dilemma."

"There isn't much quiet in a diner with the clanking of silverware, the bell above the door, the grill's sizzle, and that jukebox playing in the corner. Spit it out."

He glanced over his shoulder to look at Maddie. "That little girl was dropped off by a woman who says she's mine."

Doc furrowed his brows to the point the bushy bits touched in the center. "Her mama just dumped her in the diner?"

Alex shook his head. "Do you mind if I sit?"

Doc shoved his paper to the side. "Sit down before you fall down. You're as pale as a moonbeam."

He scooted onto the bench. "Her mother didn't

drop her off. I'm told her mother died, and her mother's friend was fulfilling a final wish."

"You're one of those musicians from Samantha's band, right?" He rubbed the white whiskers on his chin. "Does this kind of stuff happen to you guys a lot?"

"First time for me, and I'm not sure what to do. I mean, I've had women tell me they wanted my child, but this is the first time I've seen my name on a birth certificate that wasn't my own."

"Have you talked to Sheriff Cooper? He could confirm the story about the mother's death."

"Right now, I'm in shock. I'm not even sure she's mine. Can you do a paternity test?"

"Is there a possibility she's yours?" He shifted his eyes toward Maddie.

"Yes, sir. While I always used condoms, I suppose there's a failure rate to take into account."

Doc cleared his throat. "The CDC lists the failure rate at thirteen percent. In my book, those odds aren't all that good. The best way to not have a baby is not to have sex."

"That's not realistic." He could go without a lot of things, but sex wasn't one of them. Not only did it feel amazing, but it relaxed him. Sex was a part of a healthy diet, just like vegetables, sleep, and exercise. "Talking about my sex life is not why I'm here."

"Isn't it? Seems to me that's exactly why you're

sitting in my booth." He jutted his chin toward Maddie. "You don't get one of those without sex."

He couldn't argue the logic. "Can you do the test?"

"Yes, I can. It takes up to a week or so for the results to come back, but I've got a test in my clinic." He picked his paper up. "Give me ten minutes to finish Dear Abby, and I'll meet you there."

Alex moved from the booth, "Thank you, Doc."

"You should visit the sheriff first."

"I will." He took a step back.

"Son, just remember, she didn't choose you either, but you can choose how you handle it."

"Is that from Dear Abby?"

"Nope," Doc tapped his head. "That's from experience, and what you do today will follow her forever."

Alex trudged toward Maddie. Each step he took slowed with the weight on his shoulders.

"Hey, Maddie," he sat on the edge of the red bench beside her. "Those are some beautiful fish." He looked at Maisey. "Thank you for keeping her busy."

"You don't need to thank me. She's a pleasure. After you two get settled, you'll have to take her to meet Sosie. She's a local artist." Maisey held up one of Maddie's fish. "Your daughter has an eye for color."

Her words hit him so hard in the chest he sucked in a breath. There was an excellent chance she was his. Deep inside, the truth danced in his cells; Maddie was his, but what was he going to do with her?

He wasn't father material. He was on the road more than he was home. She stared at him, and he looked deep into her eyes. Eyes that somehow told him not to screw this up.

"Maddie, we need to pack up. We're going to visit the sheriff's office and then Doc."

Her eyes bugged. "No shots."

"That's right, no shots." He hoped he was right. He wasn't sure if they did swabs or blood samples. "Let me pay Ms. Maisey while you clean up your fish and crayons."

He stood and took out his wallet.

Maisey handed him the bill for his and Maddie's lunch. He paid it and gathered the folder and Maddie's suitcase. Never in his life had he considered he'd have a five-year-old.

MADDIE FOLLOWED Poppy around the office while Sheriff Cooper dug into the whereabouts of Layla Baker. He made a few calls, hung up, and took a deep breath.

The sheriff looked around. "Did they go in the back?"

Alex nodded. "Poppy took her to see the cells."

"Kids are fascinated with them. My daughter Kellyn loves to lock up her dolls when they've misbehaved." He set his hands on his desk. "Layla Baker died of a drug overdose a little over a month ago. The coroner couldn't say if it was accidental or on purpose."

Alex's hands shook. He was an adult when his mother died, and it still tore him apart. Could he have changed anything if he'd been there? That would always be the question in his mind. Then again, did his mother have much of a life? She drank and slept.

"Thank you for going to the trouble of finding out."

"What are you going to do about Maddie?"

He drew a blank. "What can I do? I'll figure out how to keep her alive until I get the results back from Doc."

The sheriff's lips stretched into a thin line.

Alex considered his word choice. "What I mean is, I'll take care of her until I get the results back. She's in no danger if you're worried."

Sheriff Cooper steepled his hands and touched his lips. "I am worried about her safety and welfare. Handing a single man a five-year-old is like asking a waitress to diffuse a bomb. It's not really in your lane. Should I call child services and have them come?

They could place her in a home until all of this is sorted out?"

The blonde's voice sounded loud and clear in his ear. *Child services should be your last resort.*

"No, I'll take care of her until everything gets straightened out. Is there anything I should be worried about as far as having her in my home? I'm listed on her birth certificate, and that makes me her father on paper, I suppose."

"You're covered. I don't imagine anyone would fault you for taking in a child that's legally yours. The only issue I see is if someone comes out of the woodwork to claim her, but the DNA test will at least tell you if there's a possibility of that happening."

"I guess I'm in a wait-and-see mode for now."

"Once everything settles down, let's get our girls together. Kellyn and Maddie are close in age, and I'm sure they would enjoy the company."

Who would have thought he'd be making playdates? "That sounds great. I'm sure Maddie would love that." Hell, he wasn't sure of anything. All he knew was he woke up this morning feeling damn good. There wasn't a naked woman on his lawn, or a pair of underwear shoved in his fence. Things were looking up until that damn bell above the door rang at the diner, and everything went to hell.

When Poppy came back, Alex held out his hand for Maddie to take. When she did, he folded his around hers until her tiny hand disappeared. He'd never been responsible for something so delicate, and yet, with all that she went through, Maddie had to be tough on the inside—like him. Hopefully, if she turned out to be his, that was something he passed on. Fierce inner fortitude would always help her during tough times.

Twenty minutes later, they had their cheeks swabbed and were on their way to his house. Buckling her into the back seat, he knew his first task was ordering her a booster seat, not because he thought about it, but because when Doc walked them out to the car, he told Alex she was too small to ride in a regular seat. Thank God for overnight shipping.

He pulled directly into the garage and helped Maddie out of the back seat. She held on to her teddy bear with one hand and took his hand with the other. His free hand grabbed her suitcase.

They walked inside and stopped in the kitchen. He wasn't sure what to call the place. To him, it was home, but to her, it was unknown. If she wasn't his, it would be a stopover. If she indeed was his daughter, he was unbelievably unprepared.

Looking at his house like it was his first time made him realize there was nothing but black, gray, and white. There wasn't a color in sight unless he counted the soda cans and beer bottles dotting the surfaces of the coffee table.

His place was hard edges and dark leather. Nothing was soft or feminine. Not one woman had graced his halls or his bed since he moved to Aspen Cove.

"Maddie, this is where I live." That sounded fine to his ears. "I'm a musician."

She cocked her head like a confused puppy. "What's a musian?"

He held back a chuckle. "Musician. Come with me, and I'll show you." He set her suitcase down and walked the hallway to his home studio. He wasn't only a drummer but a guitarist and keyboardist too. His studio had everything he needed. "I make music."

She moved with caution into the room.

He imagined it was all foreign to her, but then again, her mother was a groupie, and he wasn't sure what Maddie had been exposed to.

"Do you want to play something?"

She shook her head.

"Do you want me to play something?"

"Yeth, pwease."

He took his favorite guitar from the wall. It was the only gift his father had ever given him and was signed by all the members of Drive Shaft. Sitting on the stool, he played her an original. It was a soft lilting tune that had no lyrics yet.

Maddie sat on the floor below him, hugging her

bear and looking up with the same eyes he saw each morning in the mirror. Having a child both horrified him and warmed him. It also pissed him off. He never wanted kids because he wasn't suited to have them. He didn't want to be the kind of father his dad was—absent. And yet, if Maddie was his daughter, that's just what he was, anyway. He was a father who never visited or called or sent birthday and Christmas presents. Not that it was his fault, but kids don't know that. All they know is that you were never around.

"Do you want to try it?"

Her full, tooth-missing smile said it all.

He moved to the ground beside her and placed the guitar in her lap. It was way too big an instrument for her, so he laid it flat. If she wanted to play the guitar, he'd happily buy her one suited to her size.

She plucked at the strings, making whatever music her soul produced. Inside each person was a symphony, the music of our life. Sometimes, the notes played sharp, and sometimes they were flat, but when your soul sang in tune, it was a beautiful experience.

Maddie had an ear for music, plucking out the strings that would create a chord without thought or prodding. Her talent was raw, but he knew from her colored fish she was creative.

"That's beautiful, Maddie. Maybe someday, you'll grow up and be a guitar player."

She beamed under his praise.

How many times had he practiced with hopes to impress his father only to be critiqued or ignored? He'd never do that to his daughter. Holy hell, he had a daughter.

The next hour he let her play the drums and his keyboard. When the sun set, he cooked her a grilled cheese sandwich.

They stared at each other for endless minutes, and when he couldn't take the silence any longer, he turned on the television, found cartoons, and put her on the couch before he retreated to the studio to work on his music. When he returned, she was fast asleep, right where he left her. He covered her with a blanket, tucked her bear against her side, and headed to bed. He needed to get up early and figure out daycare.

WHEN HE WOKE the next morning, he wasn't alone. His first thought was someone had gotten past his security system unnoticed and was in his bed, but that wasn't the case. Curled next to him were Maddie and her bear.

He rolled onto his back and crossed his arms

above his head. "This is real." Somewhere in his brain, he hoped it was a dream. He couldn't call it a nightmare because the kid was too cute.

She stirred, rolled onto her back, and folded her arms above her head. "Yep."

If he weren't in such a panic about how to deal with this, he would have laughed.

"Let's get up, kiddo. How about muffins and milk for breakfast?" A trip to the bakery could solve two problems. First would be feeding the kid, and since Katie had a toddler, she'd know someone he could call. Thankfully, he'd made friends with Katie's husband, Bowie, or he wouldn't know anyone with a kid.

He sent Maddie to her suitcase to change her clothes. He'd peeked inside last night, and she had quite a few things to wear.

By the time he dressed, so had she. Fashion wasn't her thing. Nothing matched, but she was clothed.

Her hair was a whole different matter. Knotted and tangled, he had no idea what to do with it, so he raked his hands through it and used one of his hair ties.

He loaded her into the back seat and buckled her in. Her booster seat would be here that afternoon. Until then, he'd drive like a granny. When they pulled up to the bakery, sweetness filled the air.

"Let's hit it." He got her out of the car, and they walked into B's hand in hand.

"I heard a rumor," Katie said. "I didn't believe it. Thought my mother-in-law was yanking my chain." Katie rushed around the corner and squatted in front of Maddie. "How about a raspberry muffin and milk?" She ushered Maddie to a table under a corkboard labeled, "Wishing Wall" above it.

While she gathered milk, muffins, and a much-needed cup of coffee for Alex, he stared at the notes posted.

"Does anyone ever post employment needs here?"

"Sometimes, what are you looking for?" She brought their meal out and set it on the table.

"I need a babysitter."

Maddie scowled. "I'm not a baby."

Katie set her hand on Maddie's hair. "Of course you aren't. Silly men never get it right. You need a big-girl sitter."

Maddie nodded and chomped into her muffin.

"I need help with Maddie until I can figure it all out."

"I've got just the woman for you."

CHAPTER SEVEN

A sharp rap on the door saved Mercy from washing breakfast dishes. With sudsy hands, she picked up a kitchen towel and made her way to the front of her small bungalow.

She didn't get visitors unless they were bill collectors, so a knock on the door didn't bring feelings of joy. The last time someone came here, it was to deliver certified mail. Certified to drive her crazy since it was another company that wanted payment.

What she wouldn't do for a peephole. At least then, she could see who it was and decide if she wanted to answer.

At the second knock, she braced herself for the worst. "Who is it?"

"Are you Mercy Meyer?"

"Depends. Who's asking?" The voice sounded familiar, but she couldn't quite place it.

"You don't know me, but Katie from the bakery told me you needed a job, and I've recently come into a situation where I need help."

Heart soaring, she whipped the door open only to find Alex Cruz and his daughter on her doorstep. The poor kid looked like she'd been dressed by a color blind person with bad hair skills.

"Oh my God, it's you," he said.

"In the flesh." She flung the towel over her shoulder. "I could say the same. What in the heck are you doing here at my house?"

He pressed his lips together until they formed a thin line.

Maddie broke free and stepped inside. "Can I color?"

They watched her walk inside the house like she owned it. On the coffee table were cutout puppies and kittens.

Mercy used them in class for a reading project. Each time the student finished a book, they got to put an animal cutout after their name. By the end of the year, some kids wrapped the room with animals of every kind and color.

"Sure, sweetie, pick out a puppy and make it pretty." She turned back to Alex. "What do you need?"

He rubbed the scruff on his chin. Its texture sounded like sandpaper against his hand.

"Katie said you needed a job, and I need a sitter."

She looked over her shoulder at Maddie, who had made herself comfortable.

"For how long?" Inside, her tummy somersaulted because she needed a job, and this was the perfect opportunity to pay off some of her bills.

He lifted his broad shoulders, and she wondered if those muscles came from hours of drumming, or if he was born with genes that made him look like a calendar model? She would want him shirtless for June, her birthday month.

When she refocused, his mouth was moving, but she hadn't heard a word.

"Are you paying attention?"

She shook her head. "No, I was distracted. Go back to the sitter part."

His low rumble made her insides twist. "Maddie and I took the test and are waiting on the results. Doc said they should be here in a few days."

"So, you need me to watch her until you know for sure? What then? Will you toss her aside if she's not yours?" She hoped that saying it out loud made him feel like shit. However, she also hoped that Maddie didn't hear her.

When she turned, Maddie was happily playing with a dog and cat cutout.

"I can't be expected to take care of a kid that's not mine."

"Of course not, that would be too humane." She rolled her eyes. "Did it ever occur to you that she left her child to you for a reason?" While Mercy couldn't know why it seemed Maddie's mom had a plan. Most likely, it was that Alex was the father. They did have similar eyes, and both had dark hair.

"She had a reason all right. She wanted her daughter to live in the lap of luxury, where private schools weren't a problem. Where expensive clothes, vacations, and Ivy League educations were a given, but she picked the wrong guy. I'm not the catch she assumed I'd be."

"No, you're not."

He crossed his arms and spread his legs, and she swore he grew before her eyes. His stance was an intimidation technique she'd seen many times when she questioned Randy about his whereabouts. Now she recognized it as the defense mechanism it was.

"What's that supposed to mean?"

"What? I simply agreed with you."

He shook his head. "We're getting off topic. I'm here because Katie said you needed a job and I need a sitter. To me, it sounds like we're the perfect match." He closed his eyes and inhaled deeply. "What I mean is that we need each other." He shook his head and took two slow, deep breaths before looking at her. "None of this is coming out right."

"Let me help you. You don't want the responsibility of a five-year-old, and since I'm an elementary school teacher, I'm more suited to care for her while you figure out your next move."

"You're a teacher?"

"First grade. Did you think I cut out animals and sea creatures for fun? No, I do it because I know my responsibilities and want to be prepared."

"I get it; you're going to bust my balls first."

"I'd rather not talk about your balls in the vicinity of a child. In fact, I don't want to talk about them at all." With the mention of his body parts, she returned to June, and the calendar shot she'd love to see. Alex Cruz dressed in nothing except for a cute puppy placed strategically in front of him to cover his ... balls.

"Then let's talk about you watching Maddie. Layla's friend said she might be behind in her education, so having you would be beneficial."

"I'm not cheap." She had a stack of bills that said she couldn't be.

"What's it going to cost me?"

"I've got a stack of bills left by another a-hole that couldn't decide what to do about the girl, or should I say the girls in his life. They need to be paid." She didn't know what the going rate for childcare was, but her time wouldn't come low-cost. He was hiring a cook and a teacher as well as a babysitter. "It will be twenty dollars an hour."

His mouth dropped. "Are you nuts? I'm a drummer, not the star. That's eight hundred a week."

"You wouldn't play a concert for nothing, and I won't take on your child for free either." That wasn't the truth. She would have gladly helped Maddie and taken her in, but why not ask for what she needed. It was a win-win. He needed her, and she needed his money.

"I play for free often. There was the fourth of July concert, and at the end of the month, we have the Fireman's Fundraiser. I don't get paid for those."

"I'm sorry to have misspoken, but you don't want a simple babysitter. You want a tutor and a cook and a caregiver." She looked at Maddie. "She also needs a fashion consultant and hairdresser."

"You're fleecing me."

"I'm negotiating a fair wage for what you want."

She stepped forward, forcing him to move backward. "I'll be right here, Maddie. I just need a private word with your father."

"Hey," he said. "We don't know that's true. I don't want to confuse her if I'm not."

"I would imagine she's confused already. Her mother died, she's been dragged halfway across the country and shoved in front of a man who doesn't want her."

"I don't know what to do with a kid. I've never been a father."

A *pffft* sound burst from her lips. "According to Layla, you've been a father for five years and never engaged."

His face paled.

"I didn't know."

"If you had ... would you have cared?"

He raked his hand through his hair. "I can't say because I didn't know. Right now, I'm doing the best I can."

"I've found when we think we're at our best, we can always do better."

"I'm not here for an education. I'm here because I need your help. I have to be at the recording studio in less than an hour. Do we have a deal?"

If she said yes, her problems would be over sooner.

"It's a deal."

"Thank you." He turned to leave.

"Hey, don't you think you should say goodbye?"

"You're right. I'll need to practice."

She opened the door and stood aside. "To be a considerate human being? It looks like you could use some lessons in lots of things."

She hung by the door while Alex kneeled next to Maddie.

"Hey kiddo, I have to go to work. I'll pick you up later, okay?"

Maddie stopped coloring her pink cat and handed it to Alex. "Fluffy wants to come with you."

"She does, huh?"

He smiled, and the living room seemed brighter. Deep inside, Mercy knew he wasn't a bad man. He just needed a refresher course on how to be normal. Then again, how normal could a man be when he had women throwing themselves at him at every turn?

He rose and walked toward the door. "See you later, Maddie."

She lifted her head and gave him an uninterested wave. But she seemed happy, and kids generally knew what they wanted, and right now, Maddie wanted a purple dog. *At least I won't be missed.*

Mercy followed Alex out the door. "What time will you be back to get her?"

He swung around to face her. "What? Now you're my wife?"

"In your dreams, buddy. I just need to know if I should feed her."

He flushed a heated pink. "That would be great. I don't know when we'll finish recording. We're trying to complete an album so we can take the rest of the summer off."

"Good luck." She started for the door but stopped. There was a question that had been bothering her since that day in the bakery. "Hold up." She jogged to where he stood and took in his short haircut. "What's with the hair?"

He ran his hand over the short cut. "I thought it would help me blend in."

She laughed. "Keep thinking that." He would never blend in. There was something about Alex that screamed, "Look at me." She didn't know if it was his hazel eyes that switched from being bluer to more green depending on his mood or the build of a man who looked like he cut wood instead of beating sticks. It could be the smile that no doubt had melted off many pairs of panties from adoring fans. All of those things mixed with a hint of vulnerability made him stand out in a crowd.

COULD IT ALREADY BE EIGHT? She looked at the clock once more. After a full day of arts and crafts, a walk, and eating, they were exhausted. Maddie had fallen asleep with a Dr. Seuss book in her hands. Alex was right, she was behind, but she was smart, and it wouldn't take any time for her to get up to speed.

Come fall, she'd be ready for kindergarten. It wasn't hard to teach a willing student because lessons were all around them. There were colors in the garden and along the walk. Seeing wild animals was an ideal opportunity to teach her about them and nature.

She covered Maddie with a blanket and beamed down on the beautiful little girl who frequently gifted her with a smile despite her eyes staying sad. Maddie was a survivor, but Mercy wanted to make her a thriver.

A soft tap sounded at the door, and she went to let Alex in.

The scruff on his chin had thickened in the hours since she'd seen him.

"It's after eight."

"And?"

She leaned in and sniffed him to see if he smelled of alcohol, but he didn't.

"She needs a schedule. Routine is important to kids," she said in a soft tone that wouldn't wake Maddie.

"She isn't going to get that with me. I play until the gig is done."

"That's not going to work now that you have a

child." She hoped the sternness of her voice pressed past the whisper.

"We don't even know if she's mine."

She tucked her hands behind her back and clasped them tightly. It was all she could do not to slap some sense into this man.

"Regardless of who created her, she's yours for now, and that means you need to step up and do what's right for her. You can figure you out later."

"She's got what she needs."

"Hardly, when you bring her here, she needs a change of clothes, a toothbrush, a hairbrush, a favorite toy."

"I'm sorry I was unprepared. We left her bear on the couch when we rushed out to get muffins."

"But she has the other things? Like you have a toothbrush for her?" She could see by the lost look in his eyes that he hadn't considered it. "You need to shop."

A deer-in-the-headlights look froze on his face. "I don't know what little girls need."

A growl vibrated in her throat. "She needs what all girls do. Pants, shorts, dresses, underwear, sandals, tennis shoes. Her poor little pinky toe is rubbed raw on the side because her shoes are too small. She needs socks without holes and pretty hair ties. What about books and toys and a bike?"

"All of that?"

"And more. Maddie needs more."

A loud huff whooshed from his lungs. "Can you come with us? I can take time off tomorrow."

"You'll need the whole day."

"I don't have the whole day."

"Figure it out." She glanced at Maddie fast asleep on her couch. "I'll keep her tonight because it seems cruel to wake her, but you don't pay me for nights. Anything over forty hours, I get time and a half."

"I pay you enough at your hourly rate to have you twenty-four seven."

"That would cost you far more than you seem willing to invest."

CHAPTER EIGHT

At nine o'clock, Alex pulled in front of Mercy's bungalow. He hadn't taken the time to look at her home yesterday, but in the morning light, he noticed the paint peeling and a missing shutter.

By the looks of things, her neighborhood was one that hadn't been reclaimed yet. Despite the state her house was in, the manicured yard and lush flowers made it bright and homey—a stark contrast to his bungalow with a yard as austere as the interior. He had cement and dirt and a metal chain-link fence. There was nothing soft and inviting, but wasn't that what he wanted?

Something like Mercy's yard would only attract trouble. He could see it now ... women offering to be his hoe, weed *his* garden and be happy to let him fertilize theirs.

He climbed out of his car and checked the back seat to make sure he installed the booster chair correctly. When he was confident it was all right, he walked up the flower-lined walkway and knocked on the door.

Mercy opened it with a smile on her face and a cup of coffee in her hand. "Good morning, Alex." She stepped aside.

He entered a living room filled with the scent of pancakes and bacon, and his stomach growled. As a bachelor, he kept little sustenance in the house, but soda and Pringles didn't hold him over for long.

"You hungry?" She waved him forward. "You can join Maddie in the kitchen for a plate of cakes and bacon."

She led him through the living room to a small kitchen where white curtains framed the windows and looked out into another garden filled with what looked like vegetables.

"I could use a bite to eat." He took a seat next to Maddie, who didn't take her eyes off her plate. Then again, who wouldn't stare at several tiny pancakes with smiling faces made from chocolate chips?

Maddie looked content or at least put together with her hair in a fancy braid down her back. The kind of twist that started at the crown and laid flat all the way to the end.

"Two or three?"

At the sound of the question, he turned his head toward the stove where Mercy held up a spatula with a pancake hanging over the edge.

"Probably three. I imagine I'll need fuel for our shopping trip."

Light laughter filled the air, sounding like soft music coming from Mercy.

"You're probably right. I'll give you extra bacon too." She plated several pancakes and slices of bacon and set it in front of him. "Coffee?"

"Yes, please."

"Good manners are important," Maddie said with her mouth half-full.

"Yes, they are, and that means no talking with a full mouth, young lady." Mercy patted her back before taking the seat across from him and pushing his coffee forward. "Cream and sugar are right there."

He picked up the tiny cow pitcher and laughed. "Where did you get this?"

"It came with the house. I was digging in the garden one day, and it popped out of the ground. It was too sweet to toss away, so I cleaned it up, and it's been holding my moo juice ever since."

Maddie giggled. "Moo juice. That's funny."

He took his first bite and hummed. Most of his

meals were taken at Maisey's, which was as close to home cooking as he got, but this meal was different. He was sitting with a little girl that very well might be his daughter, and that would mean family meals like this could be a regular thing.

He eyed Mercy, who somehow looked softer and sweeter today. Maybe it was because they weren't arguing, which was all they'd done since they had met.

He picked up a piece of bacon and took a bite. It was perfectly crispy, the way he liked it. He could get used to this. That realization scared the hell out of him. He was not a family man, but a musician who traveled the world.

"Doesn't Maddie look pretty today?"

"She does." He glanced at Mercy, who dressed in jeans and a white T-shirt that fell off her shoulder. Would her skin be as soft as it looked?

"Time to go." He had to get out of there, or before he knew it, he'd be planning birthday parties and kitchen remodels. He gobbled down the last few bites, drank the coffee, and stood.

"Pwait in the sink, mister." Maddie pointed to where suds rose above the rim.

"Bossy thing, aren't you?"

She climbed down from her chair and put her plate in the sink.

"Go wash your hands and meet us by the door."

Sending Maddie away could only mean he was in for a stern talking to.

"What did I do now?" He asked as soon as they were alone.

Her smile threw him off-kilter. No one beamed like that before they scolded someone.

"Nothing. I wanted to say thank you for understanding that she has needs that aren't met."

He moved a step closer to her. Close enough to smell the floral perfume she wore. It was soft and smelled like garden roses. He knew the scent well because they grew wild at his childhood home.

"Thank you for helping."

She nodded toward a stack of envelopes several inches high. "It's a pleasure as well as a necessity."

"Took on more than you could afford?"

"You have no idea."

Maddie raced back and pushed him out of the way to hug Mercy. "Wets go."

"Yes," Mercy said with a giggle in her voice. "Wets go."

Alex put one hand on Maddie's head and the other at the small of Mercy's back. "What are we waiting for?" He led them through the living room, and in the short distance, the heat from touching them coursed through his veins to his heart. He swore he heard the ice inside him crack.

They walked down the path to his car, where he helped Maddie into her booster seat.

"When did you get that?" Mercy asked.

"I ordered it, and it came last night." He buckled Maddie in and reached over the seat to the passenger side to grab the bear. "Someone is missing you." He moved the bear like a puppet. "Maddie, I love you." He felt silly making a voice for the bear, but she liked it and hugged her stuffed animal close to her heart. *Was that a gift from her mom?*

"You're earning points today, Alex. You're two for two."

He opened the passenger door so Mercy could enter. "It's early yet, and I'm sure I'll mess it up somewhere."

She buckled up and turned toward him. "No doubt. You're a man, and it's inevitable."

And the Mercy Meyer with the sharp tongue was back. He rounded the corner and took a seat behind the wheel.

"Where do we go to get what we need?"

"Copper Creek will do."

He hadn't been there long enough to know his way around, so he plugged the town into his GPS, and they were off.

"Tell me about yourself, Mercy."

She turned as far as the seat belt allowed. "It's a bit late to want my resume now, isn't it? I mean, you left your kid with me overnight. I could have been a child molester."

He gripped the steering wheel so tightly his fingertips numbed. He hadn't considered any of that.

"You came recommended by someone I trust. Katie wouldn't steer me wrong."

She huffed. "Katie doesn't know me. She knows of me."

"I'm obviously unsuited to care for a child, but I'm trying."

"That's all anyone can expect."

"Educate me."

"About what?"

He had no idea what he didn't know. "First, tell me about yourself, and then tell me what you learned from spending the night with Maddie."

"Is this a post-hire interview?"

"No, I'd like to know you better."

She let out a sigh.

"I'm a first-grade teacher who works at Creek Elementary School. I've been there for a year but have been teaching for eight. I like the grade I teach because the kids are fun, still have respect for their elders, and they are like sponges."

She seemed to perk up while talking about her job. She obviously liked it.

"Where were you before Creek?"

"I worked in Silver Springs." Her words lost their lilt of happiness.

"Why did you leave there?"

Out of the corner of his eye, he watched her scrub her face with her hand. It was what he did when he was up against something tough.

"My husband died, and staying there was too painful."

His foot tapped the brake, and the car jolted like his heart. "I'm so sorry. That must be hard."

"More than you'll ever know."

"Maybe it's fate that Katie recommended you. I mean ... you and Maddie have something in common."

"Oh ... I'm certain that Maddie feels sad while my pain still sits in the rage phase."

He wasn't sure what the phases of grief were, but he knew anger was one of them.

"Everyone moves from shock to acceptance at a different pace."

She looked toward the window. "I'm pretty sure I'll stay exactly where I am for a while."

That seems odd, but what do I know? His life was different from everyone's in that he had already come to terms with his parents' loss well before they passed.

"It sounds like you love teaching."

"It's the best thing about my life. I love kids. What

we teach them now will make a difference in the world later. Everyone that Maddie comes into contact with will influence her life and mold her into the woman she'll become. What kind of woman do you want your daughter to be?"

She kept referring to Maddie as his daughter, even though it wasn't confirmed. He wasn't sure how he felt about that because he'd be a terrible role model. Hell, he was a man who used the women that used him. Not one of his concert hookups asked anything about his life or journey. All they wanted was a night of passion to write about in their journals.

"I haven't come to terms with having a little girl," he whispered. "There's no way I can imagine her as a woman."

"Keep in mind that she's going to see how you treat the ladies in your life, and that will be how she'll expect men to treat her."

"Do they still accept girls at convents?"

"You are kidding, right?"

"Well, do they?" He wouldn't want his daughter dating a musician who was never there and never faithful. Life on the road was hard, but not as lonely as others made it sound. There was always a willing woman to relieve the stress of the day. The only thing he didn't have was a confidant—someone to share his worries and wishes with. And from what he'd seen over the years, relationships were far too complicated. All he had to think about was Gray, his divorce and the settlement, to steer clear of that type of commitment.

"I'm sure they do in some places, but Maddie isn't going to be a nun. She's got so much to offer."

"I wouldn't know at this point. I don't know how to talk to kids."

"You talk to them like you would an adult. People make the mistake of baby talking to children. I find that children will rise to expectations as long as they are reasonable. No one is perfect. We all make mistakes, so expecting her to be flawless is misguided. Your first and foremost goal for her should be that she's happy."

They entered Copper Creek, and he drove down the main road where the lion's share of restaurants and shops were. "Where too?"

"Walmart is fine." She pointed to the right, where the store sat at the far side of the parking lot. "It's a one-stop shopping experience. Have you ever been in one?"

"I'm not a label snob. While I've got money, I'm not what you'd call rich."

"Rich is relative to what you have. A man who has a dollar is rich compared to the man whose pockets are empty."

He parked the SUV and helped Maddie out of the car. When she slipped her hand in his, the iciness inside him continued to thaw. It wasn't her fault that her mother was irresponsible and her father, whoever that might be, was an idiot. She'd been brought into the world, and she needed someone to acknowledge her existence.

A lump caught in his throat because, in that second, he realized that he and Maddie were more alike then different.

He swung her up and put her on his shoulders, where she held her bear with one hand and gripped his hair with the other.

"Are you ready to shop, Maddie? I hear your shoes hurt your feet."

She squealed as he spun around. Once inside, he lowered her to the cart, where she managed to squeeze her legs through the holes of the child seat. There had to be an age limit or size restriction, but he didn't care because the kid was happy and that, according to Mercy, was his goal for the day—every day for that matter.

"Let's start at shoes and work our way around," Mercy suggested. "If Maddie is a good girl, maybe Daddy will buy you a toy."

"We talked about this. Do you think it's wise to tell her something that's not necessarily true?"

She walked ahead but called over her shoulder. "Have you seen her? I mean, really looked at her?"

He had and was mostly convinced she was his

too, but until he got confirmation, he didn't want to put a title to what he was to Maddie.

"Until we know, she can call me Alex." He looked into the eyes that had watched him since they entered the store. "Okay, Maddie. You can call me Alex."

"Awex," she repeated.

It took over three hours for them to get everything Mercy thought Maddie would need, including several books, a few toys, and more hair ornaments than a show poodle, but the smiles on both of their faces were worth it.

At the checkout, the cashier gave him the total, which was less than he spent on skins for his drums.

"You've got a beautiful family," the woman with a nametag that read, Linda said.

He looked at Mercy and Maddie and realized they appeared to be a family unit. He could spend ten minutes explaining how they weren't together, but that meant ten more minutes before they could have lunch.

"Thank you."

"Your daughter favors you."

He slid his card into the machine. "She does." He decided to play with Mercy since she watched him closely, no doubt wondering how he'd respond. "But she's got her mother's disposition. It's half angel and half capuchin monkey. They're the troublemakers of the primate family."

"I'll give you trouble." Mercy took the receipt from Linda, and they moved forward. "You haven't seen trouble yet."

"I'm scared."

"Scared isn't enough, you should be terrified." Mercy raced forward with the full cart and Maddie. Once she got to a speed she liked, she stepped onto the bar of the cart and rode it with a giggling Maddie to the car.

"How about pizza?" Mercy asked as soon as they were in the car.

"Pizza," Maddie called from the back seat. "I wuv pizza."

"You love pizza. Not wuv it." Mercy turned in her seat to face Maddie. She placed her tongue to the edge of her upper front teeth and said, "La la love."

"I love pizza too." Alex said, making sure to put emphasis on the L. "Lead the way, Ms. Meyer."

She gave him directions to Piper's, and in less than ten minutes, they were in a booth waiting for lunch while Maddie played in the ball pit.

"You know those things are disgusting and full of germs, right?" Mercy pulled napkins from the dispenser and folded them in half before placing them on the paper placemats.

"But, they're fun." He glanced over to watch

Maddie dive from the side into the center and pop back up laughing.

"You'll need to bathe her when you get her home."

His heart stopped entirely and restarted with an explosion that caused the blood to pump through his veins at record speed.

"I can't bathe her. I mean ... she's a girl, and that seems wrong."

"She's your dau ... your responsibility right now, and cleanliness is important."

He shook his head. "Nope. Can't do it. I'll pay you more if you take care of that."

Mercy laughed. "You already pay me a fortune, so I'll do it now, but when she becomes a permanent fixture in your life, you'll have to figure it out. I'll see how she does in both the shower and the bath. Maybe all you'll need to do is get them ready and sit close by while she washes."

Just as his heart settled, he heard a loud cry come from the ball pit. It was a duet of unhappy kids. He took off toward Maddie to see what happened. She stood in the center next to a boy, and both were rubbing their foreheads.

He stuck his head inside the opening to the net. "Come here, Maddie. Let me see you."

She trudged through the balls, tears running

down her cheeks, and an egg forming on her forehead.

"I hit my head."

He pulled her out and held her close. "I'm sorry about that. It looks like you crashed into each other." She buried her head into his chest and bawled while he rocked her and consoled her.

Mercy stood in front of him, smiling.

"You know, anyone can make a baby. Anyone can be a father, but it takes a special man to be a daddy."

Maddie was stealing his heart while Mercy was messing with his mind. He was screwed.

CHAPTER NINE

Fridays were one of Mercy's favorite days of the week. She recharged over the weekend and was fresh for her students on Monday. Today wasn't the same as most Fridays. Once Maddie went home with her father, she'd have forty-eight hours of loneliness and no purpose.

Her phone rang, shocking her from her doldrums. Alex's name popped up on the screen. It was just after seven o'clock. Waking with the sun was the norm for her, but for a man who stayed up until the wee hours of the morning, this was odd.

Her heart skipped a beat and then another. A rush of panic crawled up her spine and squeezed her throat. Something was wrong with Maddie.

"What's wrong?" It was a rude way to answer the

phone, but she'd grown fond of the little girl and didn't want anything to happen to her. No, that wasn't right. She'd fallen head over heels in love with Maddie, and if something happened to her, it would be devastating.

"Nothing is wrong."

"Then why are you calling me at seven in the morning?"

"Because I'm tired."

Her heart pumped so hard and fast she was sure she'd keel over if she didn't get it to calm down. Air, she needed air. A fresh mountain breeze to cool the heat rushing to her face. The fragrance of lavender in bloom.

"If you're tired, then go back to bed." With her coffee in hand, she walked into her backyard and took a seat in the Adirondack chair.

"Maddie's up, and she doesn't want to sleep. Listen, she's cranky because she's missing her mother. She cried all night for her, and if I don't get some sleep, I'll never be able to record this afternoon."

She was a sucker for someone in need. That's probably why she fell for Randy. Why did she always end up with needy men? Alex wasn't hers, so it shouldn't matter, but it did. All she planned to do today was work in the garden, and Maddie could help with that.

"Can you bring her over, or do I need to come and get her."

His sigh met her ear. "I'll bring her over since I have the booster. Be there in five. And Mercy?"

"Hmm?"

"If I haven't told you lately, I appreciate all you do for Maddie and me."

"You pay me to do those things."

"I know, but you go above and beyond, and that means something."

What was she supposed to do, not feed Maddie when he ran late? Not dish him up a plate when he was hungry. She did what any decent person would do. She took care of them. On some level, they were the family she wanted but never got.

"I'll be waiting." That sounded familiar. It was typical for Randy to text and say he'd be late, and she'd always reply that she'd be waiting. Her whole marriage was spent waiting for a man who wasn't coming home.

Knowing Maddie hadn't eaten, she filled a pot of water and set it on the counter to boil for oatmeal. They could pick fresh berries from the backyard to put on top.

Just as she pulled the Quaker box from the cupboard, a recognizable rap sounded at the door. Could someone's knock be noticeable? Was it as unique as a fingerprint? No, but there was something about

Alex's that she recognized instantly. He didn't use a particular rhythm; it was more his firm touch.

When she swung the door wide, she took in the dark shadows below his eyes. Even the green in them looked tired, more like murky pond slime than emeralds. The blue was stormy instead of the color of the clear sky.

"You look like hell." She glanced down at Maddie. "But you look like a princess. Go pick out a book, and I'll read it to you while our oatmeal cooks. I want to talk to your daddy."

Maddie flung herself into Mercy's arms for a hug before she skipped toward a basket in the corner that held books for Maddie's reading level.

Alex was tired. Too tired to give her the look of frustration when she called him Maddie's daddy.

"She never hugs me."

With a roll of her eyes, she said, "Why would she? She knows how you feel. Don't think for a second that she doesn't get that temporary vibe from you." She needed to get her frustration under control. It served no one if she was angry. "What happened last night that was different?"

He leaned against the doorframe like he needed it to hold him up. "Nothing. We went home, and she played with her dolls. I turned on the TV and went into my studio."

"You left her alone all night?" Her temper flared

again. If she weren't certain he'd fall over, she'd slap him up the side of the head.

"She had cartoons to watch and toys to play with. What else could she want?"

How long could she stare at him in disbelief and remain speechless? The only word her brain formed was *you*. "She needs you." Her fisted hands remained firmly at her sides. She had never been prone to violence until she met Alex. "Imagine what she feels like. She's in a strange house with a man she's never met, and you choose music over her." She glanced at Maddie, who sat on the couch, thumbing through a *Where's Waldo* book. "Be right back, Maddie." She pushed past Alex and marched to the far end of the porch. "What the hell is wrong with you?"

"What? It's what I did when I was a kid."

"Let's give your parents an award for being loving and nurturing and creative—not. You need to do better." The last two words pinched out with so much frustration she growled.

"My parents were awful, but it's all I know."

"Then read a damn book. There's probably a million of them out there, and not one will say leave your kid alone. Imagine all the things that could happen." She stopped when she realized she'd done exactly what she was preaching not to do. She left Maddie alone, and there was a pot of boiling water on the stove.

She bolted into the house to turn the flame off and push the water out of reach.

Alex's heavy footsteps sounded behind her, and when she whipped around to face him, he smirked.

"I'm such a hypocrite, and I'm sorry."

"No, you were right. There's a lot that could happen to a kid. It's a wonder so many survive."

"I might have been right, but I was also wrong. Can you imagine what damage boiling water could do?"

"She's okay."

"This time. Maybe we both should read a book. I've never been a parent, even though it was always at the top of my bucket list. I suppose it wasn't in the cards for me."

"Did your husband not want children?"

She hung her head. "It was more that he wanted every woman but me. Sex is generally a prerequisite to procreation."

"He was an idiot."

Her shoulders lifted. "He was a man."

"Not all men are shits."

"I've yet to meet one who isn't that's not related to me." Her daddy was a perfect role model. Too bad he couldn't be bottled and sold.

Alex stumbled back, but it wasn't because of her words. He scrubbed at his eyes, and she knew he was close to collapsing.

"You'll never make it back home." She took his hand and led him through the living room and down the hall to her bedroom. "Why don't you stay here? Maddie and I are going to take a walk to the diner for breakfast." After the scare, she wasn't ready to turn up the heat again in the kitchen. "You can sleep in my bed."

His brow lifted. "You're inviting me into your bed?"

Leave it to a man to turn everything into something tawdry. "To sleep, Alex—alone."

He touched her cheek. "Your husband was a complete idiot. If you were in my bed, there wouldn't be any sleep happening."

She leaned into his touch before her common sense told her to step away. "You're in my bed, and sleep is all that happens there." She walked back to the door. "Sleep well, Alex."

Easing out of her room, she pulled the door closed behind her and clutched her chest.

Alex Cruz was in her bed. What would her mother think now?

CHAPTER TEN

Yesterday morning was the best few hours of sleep Alex had in a long time. Was it because Mercy's bed was so comfortable? Maybe it was her floral scent on the pillow that lulled him into a peaceful slumber.

"I put a couple of cookies in too," Maisey said, handing him a picnic basket. She glanced over the counter to see Maddie, who stood hugging her bear. "I'm sure Maddie will love them."

"I wuv cookies."

"That she does." He ruffled her hair. Hair that he braided poorly but should get an A for effort.

"Is Mercy going with you?" She opened one end of the basket, and the savory scent of fried chicken wafted past him. "There's far too much here for one man and a child."

He peeked inside to see chicken, fries, drinks, and cookies. Maisey added paper plates, cutlery, and napkins too.

He didn't want to start any rumors about Mercy and him. They weren't a thing, but there was no use lying to anyone.

"Yep, it appears I have a lot to learn about kids, and today is tutoring day. What better person to teach me than a teacher?"

"She's a sweet thing and pretty too."

He thought about yesterday when he asked if Mercy was inviting him into her bed. Her cheeks bloomed as red as the roses in her garden. "She seems like a good person." He refused to comment on her disposition or beauty. That would only cement the fact that he liked her, and no one needed to know that.

"Thanks for putting this together."

"No problem. You know the motto in town is 'Aspen Cove takes care of their own,' which means picnic baskets to funeral casseroles. If you're here, then you're family."

"Happy to be here." He picked up the food. "Are you ready to picnic, Maddie?"

She smiled, and it warmed his heart. Usually, her smiles were saved for Mercy, but she'd been letting them break loose here and there for him too.

They left the diner with ideas for ways to make

Maddie happy dancing through his head. After placing her and the basket safely in the SUV, his thoughts then drifted to Aspen Cove.

Weeks ago, apathy was all he could muster toward the town his boss Samantha loved so much. It didn't offer much but scenery, and there weren't any nightclubs, golf courses, or big-name grocery stores. It had the bare necessities like a diner, a bar, and a corner store. Despite his age, Doc seemed competent, and his nurse was pregnant enough to pop, even though she wasn't due for months. Aspen Cove wasn't someplace he would have sought out, but it was a place he'd like to stay—for now. What it didn't offer in amenities, it offered in charm.

They drove to Mercy's cottage and found her sitting on the steps in front. She looked downright delectable in her shorts and tank top. Why was it that he found her attractive? She was nothing like the women he took to his bed. Her hair color was natural. Her small breasts were undoubtedly nature made. The corners of her eyes crinkled when she smiled. Maybe that's what drew him to her. She was real, and if he was honest with himself, she didn't care that he was famous and didn't seem to give a damn about his money, even though she fleeced him when it came to childcare. Most importantly, she wasn't afraid to challenge him.

Then again, they weren't romantically involved.

While this seemed like a date because he invited her and she accepted, it wasn't.

He climbed out of the car and looked over the hood. "Are you ready?"

She popped up like a spring-loaded toy. A toy he'd love to play with.

"Yep." She picked up a canvas bag and slung it over her shoulder. "I packed up some toys for Maddie to play with."

She always thought ahead. He hadn't considered toys. They were going to a park where there was grass and a swing set. Who needed toys?

He walked around and opened her door so she could sit. Lavender filled his nostrils, and he immediately felt at ease. *Nope, this wasn't a date.*

At the park, they spread out a blanket and served the meal. Maddie held a chicken leg in one hand and a cookie in the other. Food was the only reason she'd willingly let go of her bear.

She was thin but healthy. Had she ever gone without a meal? He knew what that was like. He learned to cook at an early age because his mom could hardly take care of herself; she didn't have the mind to pay attention to him.

"You look deep in thought." Mercy touched his arm with her fingers. "Anything I can help with?"

He shook his head. "Just remembering my childhood."

Mercy perked up. "Did you have picnics with your parents?"

"Noooo," he drew out. "My father was absent, and my mother was a drunk. There weren't family anythings." He looked at Maddie. "That's why I'm so bad at all of this. The best way to learn is through emulation. My role models were poorly suited for parenthood."

She stared at him for a moment. "Oprah once said when you know better, then you do better. At least you recognize what you had wasn't acceptable. That makes you well suited for the parenting job because what you don't know, you'll figure out." She reached into the bag and took out a book on raising a child in the twenty-first century. "Knowledge is key."

"Is this yours?" He thumbed through the book.

"No, I bought it for you. Maddie and I went to the bookstore while you slept. We picked up more books for her." She smiled at Maddie. "She's a smart one. She recognizes new words. By the time the summer ends, if you keep me as her babysitter, she'll be reading at a first-grade level." She stuck her hand back inside the bag and pulled out *The Hungry Caterpillar.* "Hey, Maddie, when you finish eating, do you want to show your daddy how well you read?"

Maddie dropped the bone and tucked the cookie into the pocket of her sundress. "I read now."

Watching Mercy wipe Maddie's hands and face

like a mother gave him a feeling he didn't understand. It was contentment. How had a woman and child changed his life so drastically in such a short period?

He glanced at Mercy, who motioned for him to pick Maddie up and put her in his lap, and he did.

She opened the book and read. Pride swelled his heart to near bursting. When she finished, she stared at him. "That was amazing, Maddie." He looked at Mercy. "She could read before she came?"

She nodded. "Some. We're working on letter sounds, but it's hard to break habits like w to l or wuv to love. You'll have to work with her too."

Maddie climbed off his lap and ran toward the nearby slide. Watching her enjoy herself and hearing her laughter when another child slid down behind her was the simple stuff that made life enjoyable. He never thought he could sit and enjoy anything so domesticated. In Los Angeles or on the road, he was a go-go-go guy and never stopped for anything because there was never anything to enjoy. The truth hit him like a brick over the head. Fear mixed with the lies he told himself had stolen possible moments like this.

"Have you heard from Doc yet?"

Once he pushed his empty plate aside, he leaned back on his elbows. "No. I thought the results would be in, but I guess it's taking longer."

"Are you worried?"

He rolled to his side to face her. "About Maddie

being my daughter? Yes, I'm terrified, but for different reasons now."

She bit into a cookie. "Go on."

She was the only woman he'd talked to like this. Most of the women he spent time with weren't interested in his words.

"I was so certain she wasn't mine, but Doc Parker reminded me of the CDC information on condoms. The percentage of failure is really high. I thought it was about four percent, which is still high when you consider that's four out of every hundred that fail. But he said something like thirteen percent. I never worried much because most groupies were on birth control. At least the smart ones were."

"Sounds like you're getting lessons from everyone."

"No kidding. Anyway, because of my upbringing and my career, parenthood was never on my radar. I'm a fish out of water."

"Fill your tank."

She made it all sound so good—so easy.

"Don't forget, I'm a musician, and I'm on the road for months out of every year. How am I supposed to raise a little girl when I'm not around? It pretty much makes me a clone of my father, who was the lead guitarist for Drive Shaft."

"Oh. My. God. Really?"

"That's my *daddy*." Sarcasm dripped from the last word like honey from a dipper.

"Wow. I had no idea."

"Any fan worth their salt would know my whole bio. Not the parts about my mother because that's been kept hidden, but that I'm the love child of Bastian Cruz."

"Don't forget. You are not your father. You can learn from his mistakes and choose to be better." She sipped her cola. "What does Maddie call you when you're home?"

He chuckled. "She has a smorgasbord of names for me from 'hey you' to 'mister Awex.' I don't think she knows what to call me."

"Have you ever told her to call you anything specific?"

"Yes, I told her to call me Alex."

"Hmm, okay, we'll work on that. I've probably confused her by referring to you as Daddy."

"I told you that would be a problem."

"Yes, you did. Lesson learned."

"Otis," someone screamed from the edge of the park. "You get back here."

Alex saw the dog making a beeline straight toward the kids on the playground, and his heart flipped. He hadn't met Sage's dog. Though he never had a pet, he knew they could be unpredictable.

Adrenaline surged through him, and he stood

and took off toward Maddie. He got to her a second before the dog.

She clung to him like he'd saved her life. That could have been the case if Otis wasn't licking at her leg. She giggled and wiggled out of Alex's arms.

"Look, Daddy, he's a nice dog." She hugged the hound who licked whatever chicken and cookie were left on her face.

"Sorry about that." A winded Sage waddled up to him. "He's harmless."

Alex stared at Maddie, then the dog. She'd called him Daddy, and that felt strangely right.

He shook those thoughts free and shifted his eyes to Sage. "It's okay. I was worried about her for a second, but I can see Otis is harmless."

A hand settled at his back, and a sharp sense of awareness that it was Mercy rushed through him. Every time she touched him, he filled with warmth— sometimes plain old heat. The kind that got men like him in trouble—the kind that made cute little girls like Maddie.

"Any news on the test Doc did for Maddie and me?"

Sage shook her head. "You're on mountain time, and I swear slow, stubborn mules carry the mail. It'll get here in its own sweet time."

"Are you hungry, Sage?" Mercy asked. "Alex

brought enough chicken and fixings to feed an army."

She rubbed her rounded belly. "I could use a bite of something."

"You two enjoy while I push Maddie on the swings." He held out his hand, and she slipped hers into his. "You want to swing?" While they moved away, Otis abandoned them for chicken and cold fries.

For the next hour, he and Maddie played on the swings, chased each other, and tossed a ball Mercy brought. When they returned to the blanket, Mercy was grinning ear to ear.

"You're a natural."

Something had changed. She no longer looked at him like he was a buffoon, but grinned at him like he was a white knight.

CHAPTER ELEVEN

Mercy hadn't smiled that much in a long time. After yesterday's picnic, she couldn't stop.

Seeing Alex embrace his relationship with Maddie was like seeing a triple rainbow. The way he bolted from his place on the blanket to rescue his daughter from Otis, who wouldn't hurt a thing, made her heart warm.

Today she had some extra time, so she made cookies. Maddie would be upset that she didn't get to help, but eating them would ease her agitation.

As she folded the dry ingredients together, she considered her time with Alex's daughter. Though she spent hours every day with children in her job, she didn't get the opportunity to have quality one-on-

one time with them. Spending days with Maddie made her want a child of her own even more. Motherhood was another thing Randy had stolen from her.

She went about mixing the ingredients.

The eggs, butter, and oil went into the mix, and she took her frustration out on the dough. How damn selfish could a person be? He wanted his cake, which was her and everyone else's cake too. How many affairs had Randy had in their short marriage?

Her phone rang, shaking her from her mind meandering, and she reached to put it on speaker.

"Hi, Mom." Outside of bill collectors, no one else called. Then there was the ringtone that gave her away.

"Tell me about your rock star."

"He's not mine." That might be true, but it didn't mean she couldn't razz her mom. "But he did sleep here the other day?"

"You were safe, right? I mean sexually safe. You know what I always told you."

Mercy scooped spoons of dough onto a baking sheet. "I know, no glove, no love."

"That's my girl. Now give me the details."

"Oh, brother. I'm watching his daughter, and he had a rough night with her and was dead on his feet, so I told him to sleep in my bed." She didn't elaborate and say she'd been smelling his cologne since that day, so in her mind, she slept with him nightly. "I guess I didn't get your wild gene. I'm more laid-back, like Dad."

"Every relationship needs a responsible party. Your father is mine."

Mercy thought about Randy, again. She was like her father and was Randy's safe, boring place to land. She was the steady Freddy, and that was probably why he cheated on her. He loved home-cooked meals, a clean house, and pressed shirts, but he needed more in bed. She wasn't a freak in the sheets. Wax belonged in candles and rope on a clothesline.

"I'm glad you and Dad complement each other."

"Your prince will come, sweetheart. Until then, toads can be fun."

There was a knock on the door. "Maddie is here. I've got to go. Tell Dad I said hello." She started for the door.

"Honey, try to live a little. You know I'm teasing about the rock star, but don't make all men pay for Randy's misdeeds."

"I won't." She hoped that was true. How was she ever supposed to live her dream of being a wife and mother if she punished all men for another's stupidity? "Love you." She ended the call and opened the door.

Alex stood on the porch with Maddie. On his face, he had faded flowers and smiley faces. Dressed in jeans and a T-shirt, he stood in front of her wearing mismatched shoes and an endearing smile.

"Maddie picked out my clothes."

Just then, Mercy fell a little in love with Alex. She touched his cheek and glanced at Maddie. "What did you use to decorate your daddy's face?"

Maddie grinned. "Purple marker."

"Come on in. I was about to put cookies into the oven." She led them into the kitchen and pulled out a chair. "Do you want me to see if I can get that off your face?" She popped the tray in the preheated oven and set the timer.

He chuckled. "While I love the upgrade, it would be nice to have it gone." He took his phone out and pulled up his photos. "I've got it captured for posterity. I don't need to keep it in place."

Was this the same man who confronted her about the panties in the diner? No, ... this was a softer, kinder Alex.

She got Maddie started on a workbook, then went to the bathroom to get her makeup remover.

"Have a seat." She wet a cotton ball with remover and leaned in close. His cologne wrapped around her like a hug. "I like you in smiley faces and flowers. It softens your edgy demeanor."

"You think I'm edgy?"

She tilted his head to the side and wiped at a flower. "We met on less than friendly circumstances."

He smiled, and her heart stilled. "Are you ready to admit to leaving something on my fence?"

"I am not. It's not because I'm dishonest, but that I'm embarrassed. I'm not a groupie, and my mother told me to do something daring, so ... there's that."

"You need some excitement in your life?"

A smudge of purple remained that she wiped with her thumb. "As you can see, I'm a simple woman with an unremarkable life."

"I can help you spice things up."

Her adrenaline surged. Was he flirting? "What did you have in mind?" She was sure it wasn't a come-on, but the thought of doing something exciting with Alex made her ovaries dance.

"I'll figure it out." He bit his lower lip, and she was convinced that was what did it for most women he met. A gnaw here and there, and they'd be stripped down and ready for his pleasure.

"Should I be excited or terrified?"

"Maybe a little of both."

"I'm not jumping out of planes or wrestling alligators."

His low rumbling laugh vibrated the air. "No risk of that. I'm not doing either of those, but we'll find something that will get your heart racing and won't kill you."

He stood, his arm brushing against hers when he walked toward Maddie. "Hey, Mads, Daddy has to go."

She melted into a puddle watching them.

Maddie threw her arms around his neck. "I miss you."

"I'll miss you too." He stepped back. "I'll pick her up before dinner."

"Why don't you come for dinner? Maddie and I can cook something."

"Really? Should I be excited or terrified?"

"Maybe a little of both. I mean, whatever we have will be complimented by things from the garden. But Maddie is helping and thinks everything should be sprinkled with chocolate chips."

"I love chocolate-glazed carrots."

"I bet you do." The timer went off, and out came the cookies. "If you wait for a second, I'll plate you a few to take with you."

"Are you after my heart?" Another panty-dropping smile lifted his lips.

"Lord, no, I wouldn't know what to do with it." She put several warm cookies on a paper plate and passed them to him.

"Something tells me you know all about hearts."

He bent and kissed her cheek. "See you tonight, Mercy." He walked out the door.

She stood there for several seconds until Maddie pulled on her sleeve. "Can I have a cookie?"

"You bet."

Once Maddie had her cookie and milk, Mercy put the remover away and planned for the day.

THIS WASN'T A DATE, but she was as nervous as a teen on prom night. She checked her hair twice. Since she licked her gloss off once already, she slicked on another coat.

When he tapped on the door, her heart dropped into her stomach. On the way to the door, she chastised herself for thinking the dinner was anything more than a kind gesture. She invited him, not the other way around.

"Maddie, your Daddy is here."

She raced from the kitchen to the door. "Do I look pretty?"

Someone else was after Alex's heart. It was heartwarming to see how much they bonded in the short time Maddie had been here.

"You always look pretty." Mercy braided her hair and worked a few small daisies into it.

She swung open the door, and Alex stood with matching shoes and two bouquets.

"These are for my favorite girls." He handed the gerbera daisies to Maddie and the larger bouquet of mixed flowers to her.

How long had it been since she received flowers? Smelling them filled her with giddiness.

"Thank you, Alex. Are you hungry?"

"Starving. What are we having?"

She walked to the kitchen and rummaged under the sink for mason jars to put the flowers in.

"I thought we'd grill chicken and serve it with a salad Maddie and I made from things I grew in the garden."

"I can grill."

"You grill?" She couldn't imagine him doing something so domestic.

"I cooked a lot when I was a kid, and barbecuing was my favorite because it created fewer dishes to wash."

"You were wise for a kid."

"I think it was laziness back then, but now I try to work smarter and not harder. Is the grill out back? I'll get it ready if you're okay with that."

"That would be awesome. The yard is fenced, so Maddie can play out there."

"Come on, Mads, let's barbecue."

Maddie skipped beside Alex like she was always

there by his side. He stepped up to the challenge of parenthood quickly, despite his arguments.

She put everything she needed for their dinner on a tray and walked out the back door to find the barbecue lit and Maddie walking Alex around the yard. She pointed out all the vegetables and fruits she learned that afternoon.

This was a little piece of the Walton's or Mayberry that she always wanted but never got.

Heat poured off the barbecue, burning anything on the grill, but to make sure it was clean, she took the scraper and moved it across the grate.

"That's not your job." Alex raced toward her and squeezed in close before taking the scraper. "You worked all day, let me grill the chicken." He nodded toward the table. "You sit."

"Do you want a beer?"

He shook his head. "No, but a glass of water would be great. If you tell me where to go, I can get it myself."

"I'll get it for you while you cook the chicken."

Back with the glass of water, she called Maddie over to wipe her hands before asking her to serve the salad. Maddie liked helping, but that didn't surprise her because most people wanted to feel needed and valued.

After plating the chicken, they sat down for dinner together.

"Do I have a grandma?" Maddie tucked her legs under her body and leaned toward Alex.

His expression was thoughtful, as if weighing his words. "Your grandmother and grandfather have both passed away."

"Are they in heaven with Mommy? Maybe they can take care of her."

Mercy swallowed the lump in her throat. "I'm sure they will." What five-year-old asked that kind of question? No doubt, one that did a lot of caring for someone else.

Alex gripped his silverware so hard that Mercy was certain he'd leave dents in the metal. "It's like an endless loop. For every poor decision we make as adults, there's a kid that pays the price."

She laid her hand on top of his and rubbed gently across his knuckles until the tension faded.

"I never wanted ... you know, and this was why. No child should have to do what I did, and it bothers me that Maddie went through it."

"Life was pretty darn good to her if you ask me. It gave you to her. She's a lucky girl to have someone who has been through what you have and come out the other side. You have something inside that few people do—perspective."

They looked at Maddie, who picked the strawberries from her salad and pushed the lettuce aside.

"You need to eat it all if you want banana pudding."

"Banana pudding with vanilla wafers?" Alex rose in his seat, and she imagined him as a child. The exuberance over pudding and cookies charmed her.

"And whipped cream."

He closed his eyes and looked to the sky. "I found nirvana, and it's in a small town named Aspen Cove. I'm starting to see why Samantha loves it here."

"That's easy; it's because Dalton's here and love makes you do crazy things ... even move to a speck of a town in the Rockies."

She coaxed Maddie into two more bites and gathered the plates. When she came out with the trifle bowl full of pudding, they clapped.

With bellies full and everyone happy, Maddie went inside to sit on the sofa and read a book while Alex helped clean up.

"Thank you for helping." She wiped her hands on a towel and took a few steps toward the living room and Maddie when Alex reached out and stopped her.

"Mercy ... I don't know how to properly thank you for all you've done. You have been a wonderful influence on Maddie and me."

She was close enough to see the specks of gold in his eyes.

"It's my job."

He shook his head. "No. It's more than that. I can hire you for babysitting, but I can't pay someone to care, and it's obvious that you do."

His proximity did crazy things to her body. Unlike her mother, she'd never been a groupie, but she was a real fan of Alex, not the musician but the man.

"She's amazing, and so are you." Her chin dropped. "It's been my pleasure, and in the short time she's been here, she's blossomed."

"You're making a difference in our lives."

"And you in mine."

He moved closer. " This might be a weird question, but can I kiss you?"

"Me? Why me?" She looked behind her expecting to see someone else.

"Why not you?" He ran his thumb down her cheek as he inched closer to her face.

"Because I'm me."

His lips brushed against hers. "And I like you."

"Well then, you better kiss me."

She expected a crash of lips and teeth, but the kiss was slow and sweet. She no longer had to wonder what his lips would be like on hers— this was *her* nirvana.

"That was perfect," he said against her lips. When he stepped back, he looked at her like she was the only woman in the world. "Since you made me dinner, how about I take you out for a meal?"

Her heart filled with fear and excitement. What was happening with them?

"Are you asking me on a date?"

He bit his lower lip, and when it popped free, he said, "Yes, I believe I am."

"It's a date then."

His lips touched hers briefly. "Friday? I'll arrange for a sitter."

"We can bring Maddie."

He shook his head. "It's a date, and that means two people having a nice time together."

"Okay." Energy pulsed through her. "What should I wear?"

"If it were up to me, you'd wear nothing, but something casual nice will do."

Her cheeks heated. What the hell was casual nice? "I haven't been on a date in years."

He rubbed his chin. "I don't think I've ever been on a real date."

She lifted her brows. "You should know, I don't put out on the first date."

He laughed. "Neither do I."

"You're such a liar." She tapped him on the arm with a fist.

"Seriously. I'm telling the truth. I haven't ever put out on a first date. Maybe that's only because I have never been on one." He touched her lips again in a brief fly by. "I'm looking forward to you being my first, Ms. Mercy Meyer."

They walked into the living room where Alex hoisted Maddie to his hip, and after a wave goodbye, they left. The only thing that proved the night was real was the half-eaten bowl of banana pudding and the tingle on her lips.

CHAPTER TWELVE

Since Samantha wanted to finish the album so they could have downtime between its completion and the Fireman's Fundraiser, there wasn't much time to indulge, and Alex didn't think there were enough kisses between the barbecue and his date with Mercy on Friday. They were working long hours, and by the time he picked Maddie up, he was exhausted. All he could do was take her home and spend quality time until it was her bedtime.

But now that Friday was here and he managed to get a sitter, he was revived and ready to go.

"Are you sure you have everything you need?" he asked Louise.

"Honey, I've got eight kids, if I don't have it, they don't need it."

He watched Maddie cautiously approach some of Louise's brood.

"Do you think she'll be okay?"

She looked over her shoulder and laughed. "She's fine. I haven't killed one yet, not that I haven't been tempted. Give her five minutes to warm up to the girls, and they'll be fast friends. Are you sure you don't want her to spend the night? We're happy to keep her."

While a night with Mercy sounded tantalizing, they weren't moving that fast. She was different. Maybe he liked her because she wasn't like the rest. Her expectations weren't the same, and he wanted to aspire to be the man she thought he was. The way she looked at him made him feel better than the playboy he'd been. For Maddie and her, he'd do better.

"I'll be back by nine to get her. Mercy says a consistent schedule is good for Maddie."

"Without a schedule, you don't have a life." Louise laughed. "You don't think I have eight kids because the little ones stayed up all night, do you?"

He stepped back. "I'm not ready for more."

"Problem is, they multiply like rabbits. You start with two, and before you know it, you've got a fluffle."

"A what?"

"Lots of cute little bunnies. Now get and have a

good time. Maddie is going to have the time of her life. It's s'mores night, and that's one sticky chocolatey mess."

He backed up a few feet before turning away.

"Don't forget flowers because most women are a sucker for them. You might get lucky if you show up with a bouquet."

He chuckled. "You know what? I'm already lucky just to have this date."

"You're a smooth one."

He waved and walked down the sidewalk. "Call me if you need me."

He climbed into his SUV and headed to the corner store. This parenting thing was hard. There was so much to consider, but the dating thing really had him stumped. Was it wise to bring her flowers twice in one week? Would she think he was angling to get between her thighs? He was, but not for simple sex. He'd be in Aspen Cove for the time being and having someone to share his life with looked appealing.

He parked between the corner store and the pharmacy, knowing flowers couldn't hurt. His mom used to buy them and say they were from his father. Somehow, the lie made his abandonment less painful.

Just as he reached for the handle, Doc called his

name. The older man waved an envelope above his head while he ambled forward.

"Came today. I was going to drop it off at your place, but since you're here, thought I'd save myself the trip." He placed the paternity test in his hand.

Why did his heart beat wildly like an animal trapped in a cage?

"Thanks, Doc."

"Well, are you going to open it?"

It sat like a snake in his palm, ready to bite. As soon as he opened it, his life would change. If Maddie was his, that meant more changes were coming. What happened when they went on tour? How would she get to school and home each day? Who would watch her once summer ended and Mercy went back to work? If she wasn't his, what did that mean? Every time she called him Daddy, his heart danced. Who knew the one thing he avoided his entire life—fatherhood—could bring him such joy? "Eventually. Right now, I'm picking up flowers and then my date."

Doc set his hand on Alex's shoulder. "Son, no matter the results, just remember that DNA don't make a daddy."

That was the awful truth. "I know." He lifted the envelope. "Opening this will only confirm what I know in my gut. Maddie's mine."

"She was yours the day you decided that to be true. Enough about that, go get your date."

Alex folded and shoved the envelope into his pocket and strode into the store. Things were changing all right; he had a house, a daughter, and a date.

He entered the Corner Store and walked into some kind of negotiation. The older couple who owned the store shook hands with a woman.

"End of the month, then?"

"You'll get the keys."

He moved to the front where buckets of water held flowers. He took all they had and placed them dripping on the counter.

"Looks like you either screwed up or you're sucking up," the man said.

"Neither, it's date night."

The younger woman cocked her head to the side. "Are you the drummer for Indigo?"

He wasn't in the mood for fan behavior, so he pointed to his hair. "I'm not that guy." Not anymore.

"You look just like him."

He paid his bill and picked up the flowers.

"They say everyone has a doppelganger." He studied her for a moment. "You look like that girl from a beer commercial."

"I get that all the time, and if it brings more people

into the Corner Store, I'll pretend I'm her and sell autographs." She held out her hand for a shake. "I'm Jewel, and I take over this fine establishment next month."

He nodded. "Nice to meet you." He pivoted on his heel and fled before anyone else could waylay his progress. If he didn't get to Mercy's soon, she might think he wasn't coming.

———

THEY SAT at a small table in Trevi's Steakhouse in Copper Creek. The soft murmurs of couples talking mixed with the smell of garlic and spices. The dim, romantic lighting made the place perfect for a first date. He'd have to thank Dalton for the suggestion.

Mercy sipped her glass of wine while Alex drank a soda. He rarely imbibed because he'd once read that addictive personalities ran in families, and he worried he'd end up with the alcoholic gene.

"You didn't have to buy out the store." She set her glass down. "Right now, there's a wife somewhere thinking ... where are my flowers?"

"I couldn't choose and realized I didn't have to. I'm learning that I can have it all, so why shouldn't you have every flower?"

"I bet you made Phillip and Marge happy with the sale."

"If not them, then the new owner."

"There's a new owner?"

"I walked in on the handshake. The new owner is a woman named Jewel."

She fidgeted with her silverware and rearranged her glasses for the third time.

He touched her hand, covering it with his. "Are you nervous?"

"No. Yes." She took in a long, deep breath and huffed it out. "Okay, I'm worried."

"About?"

She pointed to him and back to her. "This. What is it? Where is it going? I keep asking myself if I'm stupid to think you'd be interested in me when you have so many beautiful women leaving you sexy lingerie." She lowered her head. "Is she pretty?"

He squeezed her hand. "Is who pretty?"

"Jewel. Even her name is alluring."

He slid his chair closer. "I didn't stay around long enough to look." He'd never tell her she looked like a beer commercial model because that was irrelevant. The only person who grabbed his attention was Mercy. "I had this hot date with a sexy schoolteacher."

"You're just saying that because you want to get lucky tonight."

He lifted her hand to his lips and left a lingering kiss on her palm. "I have it on good authority that's not happening, so the thought didn't cross my mind when I said you were beautiful."

"Liar."

"About you being beautiful ... no way, as for the getting lucky, a man can dream."

Their dinner arrived. He had the ribeye, and she had the filet. They ate and talked.

"What's it like being you?" she asked.

He finished his bite and swallowed. "It's not as sweet as you'd think. No one ever takes the time to know you as a person because all they want is a piece of you. A check mark on their list of things to do in life."

"But all these women fall in love with you."

He shook his head. "Not with me, but with who they think I am, and what they think I can offer. It gets old after a while."

"I bet it does. While I'm no musician, I know what it feels like to be marginalized. Randy, my deceased husband, loved that I cleaned and cooked and did laundry, but he ..." She swallowed hard, and he worried she would choke on the words. "He obviously didn't think I was good in bed or his tastes were different than what I offered because he cheated." Her eyes grew wide. "You're the second person I've ever told, but did you hear that story about the man who got his ... you know ... bit off in a car accident?"

"Who hasn't, it was international news." His eyes grew wide. "That was your husband?"

Her lips pressed into a thin line. "It was so embarrassing."

"His stupidity is not a reflection on you. He was an idiot for cheating and a bigger one for getting his dick bit off."

Something worried her. He saw it in the way her eyes dulled.

"Maybe it all comes back to me. If I'd been better for him, he wouldn't have had to look elsewhere."

If Randy weren't already six feet under, he'd be happy to send him there. "Did you wait until marriage before you had sex?" He didn't want to call it making love because thinking about Mercy loving anyone but him didn't sit right.

"No. I'm not a prude."

"You certainly don't kiss like a prude. Was the marriage sex good?"

"I thought it was good for him. I mean ... he always ... you know."

"But did you?" Part of him wanted her to say never because that meant he'd be able to give her something her former husband didn't or couldn't.

"There was one time, but it seemed like a fluke."

He wanted to throw his fists in the air, but she didn't need his arrogance. What she needed was his reassurance.

"It wasn't you. Some men don't know when they have a good thing. They ruin it searching for something better, but it's rarely out there."

"Is that what you did? Were you looking for something better?"

He shook his head. "No, I wasn't looking for anything until I found you."

CHAPTER THIRTEEN

Mercy nearly swooned at that statement. Alex Cruz was one smooth operator.

"I bet you say that to all the girls."

He sat back and seemed to study her. With a shake of his head, he said, "Nope, I've only said it to you, but there's one other girl I could say it to, and the words would hold."

Her heart sank. For once, she would like to be the only one. "Maybe you should tell her."

He grinned. "Are you jealous?"

Yes, she was. It was a ridiculous emotion. You either had the heart of a man, or you didn't.

"No, I'm not."

"Liar."

She rolled her eyes. This was becoming their

game, but she'd play along. "Okay, it's not that I'm lying, it's that I'm embarrassed to admit that I like you more than I want to."

He lifted a brow. "You don't want to like me?"

"I already like you. It's trust that I'll struggle with."

"My career isn't the kind that will give you peace of mind, but don't bury your heart with your dead husband."

He was right, and she knew it, but how could she trust a man who had a string of groupies at every venue?

"Look, I'm making more of this date than it probably is, and I apologize."

He took her hand in his. "Though I'm not ready to buy the ring, this is a real date. Not a ploy to get you naked and in my bed. If I just wanted someone between the sheets, I don't need to wine and dine them. I've got twenty new lingerie pieces to prove it, but you know which are my favorite?"

"I don't want to know."

"Yes, you do, because they are a pair of pink cotton panties."

She pulled her hand away and covered her face. "So embarrassing."

"So cute." He waved the waiter over to pay the bill. "I hate to cut our date short, but I've got the other girl I didn't know I was looking for until she found me, waiting. She has a strict bedtime, or she gets cranky."

As fast as her heart sank, it rose like pretty colored helium balloons were attached to it.

"Maddie is a lucky girl."

"Nah, I think it's me who's lucky. You don't know what you're missing until you get a taste of what you never had."

"Sounds like a country song."

"Not yet, those almost always come with broken hearts, and I'm not planning on breaking any in the near future."

If that wasn't swoon-worthy, she didn't know what was. Thankfully, the chair had arms she could grip, or she would have been in a puddle beneath the table.

As soon as the check was taken care of, Alex held her hand and walked her to the valet. While they waited for the SUV, he kissed her like every word he'd said during dinner was real. Could a heart as fractured as hers ever mend? She hoped so because love was all she ever wanted.

TUCKERED OUT BUT HAPPY, Maddie ran to the door when they arrived at Louise's.

Alex had planned to take her home first, but

Louise's house was on the way, so they figured they'd get Maddie and then take Mercy home, but once in the car, Maddie begged Mercy to come to their house and tuck her in. When those hazel eyes looked into hers, she couldn't say no.

He led her inside to a living room of black and metal and glass. There wasn't color around unless Maddie's one-eyed tan bear counted.

Alex's house was as warm as an ice cube and as inviting as a barbed-wire fence.

"I know, it's like entering a black pit."

"That's being kind." She moved around the perimeter, skimming her fingers across the empty bookshelves. "Do you have pictures or stuff you've collected along the way?" Maddie tugged on her hand. "Come see my room."

Mercy said a silent prayer that Maddie's room wasn't as unwelcoming and sighed in relief when she entered and found a toy box full of dolls and a bed made but covered in stuffed animals. There was nothing on the walls except for a purple flower and a smiley face drawn in marker.

"I see she's beat you to the decorating."

"I'm at a loss when it comes to making the place homey. I'm rarely anywhere more than a few weeks."

That was a grim reminder that Alex wouldn't make Aspen Cove his permanent residence. And what would he do with Maddie? Would she get boarded out during the school year, or would he hire some cute little French au pair to take care of all his needs?

"You okay?"

She pushed her thoughts aside. "Yes. Fine."

Alex slung his arm over her shoulder. "One thing I know for sure is that fine is never actually fine. You want to talk about it?"

"There's nothing to talk about." She walked deeper into Maddie's room. "Where are your pj's kiddo? It's time for bed."

Maddie attempted to snap her fingers. "Dang it. Can't I stay up with you?"

"Not a chance, Mads, you need to get some sleep if you want to have breakfast at Maisey's before I go into the studio."

That got her moving. Maddie took her Disney Princess pajamas from her dresser and changed. With a tug, she dragged Mercy into the bathroom.

"Look at my toofbrush. It plays music."

Alex put a dab of toothpaste on it and pressed a button, making the music start.

"She brushes until the music shuts off."

"That's awesome." Mercy loved that he dove headfirst into parenting. "Where did you get that?"

"Amazon, where I get everything else I never knew I needed, like more hair ties." He opened the bathroom drawer to show at least twenty different types. "This looks full now, but by next week there won't be one anywhere. It's like they evaporate overnight. Who knew girls were so expensive?"

"They don't have to be."

"Oh, please. Boys need tennis shoes, shorts, jeans, and T-shirts. Girls need everything. There are dresses and skirts and sandals and tennis shoes and hair ties and barrettes."

Mercy's shoulders shook with her laughter. "Okay, I get it. Girls need more."

Maddie's toothbrush stopped singing, and she opened to show Alex her teeth. "Into bed, Fred." He patted her bottom, and she laughed.

"I'm not Fred; I'm Maddie."

"Yep, and it's past your bedtime."

Maddie ran to her bed and jumped on top, and after a few bounces, she climbed under the blankets. "I'm ready."

Mercy cocked her head to the side. "Do you read her a story every night?"

"No, we have our own thing. I'll be right back."

Mercy sat on the edge of the bed and tucked the blankets in around Maddie. This was the dream.

"Did you have fun with the Williams' kids?"

"Yes, I want to go back and play. Do you think I can go tomorrow?"

"You're staying with me tomorrow because your dad is trying to finish a project so he can spend more time with you, but maybe we can get Louise to bring the kids to the park. Would that be fun?"

"Yes."

Alex returned with his guitar and stood by the bed. "You play her music?"

"Every night." He moved to the end and sat on the corner. "I wrote this song for Maddie."

He strummed a chord and started to sing. And boy could the man sing.

Your chestnut hair, and your soulful eyes.
They sing to my heart.
A tiny nose, and a toothless grin.
They sing to my heart.
Your trust and your love.
They sing to my heart.
Little girl of mine
You have my heart

The song continued for several verses, and when Alex finished, Maddie was asleep, and Mercy was in tears.

They moved slowly out of her room and closed the door behind them.

"You okay?"

"I'm perfect."

"That's a hell of a lot better than fine." He walked her into the living room, where he leaned his guitar against the wall.

"I didn't know you played the guitar or that you sang."

"There's a lot about me you don't know." He sat and pulled her into his lap.

"Tell me more. I want to know Alex the man, not only Alex the sexy drummer from Indigo."

"Sexy, huh?"

"You know you are. You have your own fan club."

He situated them so her legs rested on the couch, and her back leaned against the armrest.

"None of that matters to me. All I care about right now is how you feel about me."

"If I'm on the fence, will you write me a song?"

His hand settled on her thigh, and a sizzle burned through the cotton fabric of her dress to her core.

"You want me to write you a song?"

"Seriously? Yes, I want a song. Will you tuck me into bed each night and sing it to me?"

"The logistics are tricky, but I'm sure we can figure something out." He cupped her cheek and pulled her in for a kiss. When he leaned back, she saw eyes darkened with passion. "Stay the night with me."

"I can't. It's too soon."

He nodded. "I understand." Disappointment oozed from his words.

"Do you?"

He nodded. "Yes, you're different from the rest. You're not a one-night stand. You want more."

"I'm not sure what I want, but this is enough for now."

It would be easy for her to say yes to a night of passion, but what would be left in the morning? Her body screamed full speed ahead, even her brain was on board, but her heart put on the breaks.

They kissed for the better part of the next hour. Alex risked a squeeze of her breast, and that's when she knew she needed to go because if she didn't leave now, she'd be naked and in his bed within minutes.

"I need to go." He let out a slow, sexy groan that nearly changed her mind. Did he make the same sound when he made love? She closed her eyes and pictured him nude, braced above her body, arms flexed, muscles taut. "Holy hell. I ... I've gotta go." She hopped off his lap and took several steps back. Alex was as hot as a flame, and wasn't it dangerous to get too close to the fire?

"But someday you'll stay, right?"

"That might send the wrong message to Maddie."

"What message? That I care for you and I want to make love to you? It's not like I'm going to lay you on her twin bed while she sleeps. We can be discreet."

"Discreet just sounds like a dirty little secret. I've had enough of those in my life."

His sigh came out a half breath and half growl.

"I'm going to change your mind about men, about me, and about staying the night." He lifted from the sofa and retrieved his key from the entry table. "Take my SUV. I don't want you walking home alone."

She took the keys from his hand and moved to the door where he kissed her once more.

"Just so you know, I want to stay, but I know I shouldn't."

He walked her to his car and opened the door. "I know you shouldn't, but I want you to stay too. Next date, Maddie will have a sleepover, and so can we. No pressure, just think about it."

She adjusted the seat and mirrors and backed out of his driveway. All the way home, she couldn't think about anything else.

CHAPTER FOURTEEN

When morning came, Alex flopped onto his back and stared at the ceiling. He tossed and turned all night, thinking about Mercy and her kisses, and he was exhausted. If one of her kisses touched his soul, then what would making love to her be like?

The lack of sleep made his limbs heavy, and he climbed out of his bed and slogged toward the shower. His jeans, which he'd discarded in the corner of the room last night, caught his attention. Or the letter peeking out of his back pocket did. How could he forget the test?

He bent over and swiped the envelope, turning it over and over while his stomach churned. What if Maddie wasn't his? What if she indeed was?

He moved into the bathroom and set the envelope on the counter. Whatever was in it could wait until he was fully awake, and the only thing that brought him out of the fog of slumber, restless or not, was water, steam, and soap, followed by coffee.

The letter sat heavily in his consciousness while he moved through his morning routine. Up until now, things had been easy. He had Mercy watch Maddie, and all he was responsible for was hanging out a few hours with her at night and playing a song for her at bedtime. The hard stuff was in Mercy's hands. She was the one who entertained Maddie during the day. She fed her lunch and dinner and often bathed her before he picked her up. She made lists of things for him to purchase, like books and educational toys.

He had so many deliveries, the UPS man knew him by name and vice versa. Alex's house was his first and sometimes only stop in Aspen Cove. Thank the heavens for Prime shipping.

Yep, he had it easy.

Once out of the shower, he dried, dressed, and picked up the envelope. Passing Maddie's room, he found her playing with her dolls and leaned against the doorframe to watch.

Watching her play gave him great insight into her childhood. Had he been so easy to read while playing with his action figures? Did he lay them down and pretend he couldn't wake them up?

"But, Mommy, I'm hungry." Maddie shook her doll—the crazy American Girl doll that looked just like her. It wasn't something Mercy suggested he buy, but when he did a search for dolls every young girl wanted, he came up with the brand, and once he saw Samantha, he knew he needed to buy it. Not only was that his boss's name, but the lifelike doll looked insanely similar to his daughter. He was even able to customize the eyes, so they were blue-green hazel.

He stepped forward.

"Go away, Maddie, I'm tired."

He paused to see how this would play out.

"But, Mommy."

"Later, there are Pop-Tarts in the cupboard."

That nearly broke his heart. If this was a reenactment of her life, then history had repeated itself for his daughter. He lived off of toaster pastries and peanut butter sandwiches for years. That's why he learned how to cook.

Not wanting to startle her, he stepped back and knocked on the doorframe. "Hey, Mads, are you hungry?"

She spun around to face him. Her somber expression faded, and a smile lifted the corners of her lips.

"Yes."

"Do you want cereal here or pancakes at Maisey's?"

"Oatmeal. I want oatmeal."

He scrunched his nose. "Really?" What kid willingly ate oatmeal?

"Oatmeal, it is. Do you need help picking out your clothes, or do you want to dress on your own?"

"Dress myself." She ran over to the chest of drawers and dug through them to find what she wanted.

"Don't forget to brush your teeth. Meet me in the living room in five minutes, and I'll do your hair."

He watched no less than a dozen YouTube videos on braiding hair, and while he couldn't figure out the french one, he got pretty good at a simple braid.

He stuck a K cup in the maker, and while it brewed, he slid a finger under the flap to open the test results.

Maddie raced into the kitchen, wearing an interesting combination of plaid and florals and a glob of toothpaste on her lower lip.

"I weddy."

The pot stuttered to a finish, and he grabbed his mug. It seemed as if the universe was dead set against him reading the results, so he tucked the envelope into his pocket once again.

If he were lucky, he'd have time for a few sips of coffee while he fixed her hair.

He led her into the living room, where she sat on his lap while he perfected his coifing skills. When he finished, he admired his work. Today, he managed to get them even.

"Let's go, princess." Since Mercy had his SUV, they were on foot.

"Daddy, I'm not a pwincess; I'm just Maddie."

He tickled her sides. "You're my princess, Maddie, and I love you." He stilled at the words that slipped so easily from his lips. He hadn't said them to anyone other than his mother, and yet, they felt so right. This little munchkin had wheedled her way into his heart in no time at all.

———

AT MAISEY'S, they took a booth to the left next to Doc's, who hid behind his newspaper.

"What are you two up to?" Maisey asked.

"Late breakfast, and then I'm off to the studio while Princess Maddie goes to Mercy's."

"I heard you two are dating." Maisey leaned a hip on the booth and took out her order pad and pen.

"We went to dinner. With all the things Mercy does for Maddie and me, I thought it would be nice to have a night out."

"Mmm-hmm. Just being nice, huh?" She lowered herself so she talked to Maddie face-to-face. "What's it going to be, Princess Maddie?"

Maddie giggled. "Oatmeaw with wayzins and sugar and mook."

"And for you, Mr. Just Being Nice?"

"Pancakes and sausage."

"Coming up." She pivoted and walked away.

Doc lowered his paper. "Morning, Alex. Maddie."

Maddie got on her knees and turned to face him. "You got a wifesaver?"

Alex chuckled from the memory of Doc Parker swabbing Maddie's cheek for the test, and when she opened her mouth to say something, he popped a cherry Life Savers inside. Alex wasn't sure if it was a treat for behaving or a way to keep kids' mouths busy, so they didn't chat his ears off.

Luckily for both of them, Maddie wasn't much of a talker. He was sure that came from being on her own a lot. Like him, she had to learn to entertain herself, and talking to no one was never all that much fun. Then again, he didn't have a Samantha doll growing up.

"I do not. Besides, you don't want to spoil your breakfast." His eyes lifted to Alex. "Did you open the envelope?"

He'd almost forgotten about it again. Reaching back, he plucked it from his pocket and held it in the air. "Got it here. Last night was—"

"Date night. I heard."

"Sheesh. Nothing gets by anyone here."

"Your SUV is parked in front of Mercy's place. I'd say that was some night."

He hadn't thought of ruining Mercy's reputation if his car was seen in front of her place all night. In a small town, nothing went unnoticed.

"She didn't stay the night. We went to my place, and once I got Maddie to bed, I couldn't leave her alone, so I gave Mercy the keys."

Doc rubbed at his bushy brows. "Proud of you, boy. It's the things we have to wait for that mean the most." He leaned back and sighed. "Take my Lovey, for instance. I noticed her right away. For years we square-danced together. I only went because square dancing was on my wife Phyllis's bucket list, and we never got around to it. I took her list after she passed and lived vicariously through her. Little did I know that Phyllis's desires would turn into a dream come true."

Alex was trying to follow along. "Phyllis was your first wife?" He'd seen Doc and Agatha together and thought they'd been a couple for life.

"Pay attention, son. I was married to Phyllis for forty-plus years. We had Charlie together. She's the vet here in town."

The pieces were coming together. It seemed as if somehow most people were related in some way, either by marriage or DNA. He gripped the envelope more tightly before setting it on the table.

"So, you met Agatha and got a second happily ever after?"

"Sure did. That woman was relentless, but I wasn't going to rush things. I didn't want to bring a new woman into my life when I wasn't sure if I'd gotten over Phyllis, but then I realized that I'd never get over my first true love."

"Is there a lesson here?" Doc seemed to offer advice like he did medicine—in measured doses.

"All I'm saying is the heart always has room for more, but don't rush into filling it. Racing to the finish line doesn't always make you a winner."

"I'm not in a rush for anything."

"There's a risk for going too slow too. The tortoise might make it to the finish line, but if he's too slow, what will be left when he gets there?"

Maisey swooped to their table with hands full and dropped off their breakfast.

Alex forked a piece of sausage. "Don't rush, but don't go too slow. Are we talking about Mercy or Maddie?"

Doc lifted his shoulders. "I'm an old man. I'm just talking. All I'm saying is listen to your heart, it will know. I'm also saying that time has value, and when you put time into something, it's worth more. Then again, if you wait too long, it might be worth nothing."

Doc folded his paper and placed a five-dollar bill on the table before he got up. "Have a good day, you two." He nodded to the envelope. "Another thing. Don't let a piece of paper define life for you. You get to choose, or at least your heart does." He walked away.

Alex sat there for a long moment, wondering what the hell Doc had just told him. His words were opposites. Take time ... don't. Love her now ... wait. He was confused, but one look at Maddie clarified everything. She needed him now, later, and every minute in between. His heart told him he had no choice. Maddie was his, and he'd do right by her.

After several bites of his pancakes and sausage, he set down his fork and picked up the envelope.

Rather than gently peeling back the flap, he tore it open and unfolded the letter. As he read through the test results, his heart stilled.

Maddie Cruz was only his in name. She didn't share any of his DNA.

He stared at her for several minutes. She had his eyes, hair color, and swore when she smiled, his dimple puckered on her cheek. How in the hell couldn't she be his?

Gone was his appetite, and back was the knot in his gut.

Maisey walked by with the pot of coffee swinging between her fingers. "Something wrong with the cakes?"

He shook his head. "No, I wasn't as hungry as I thought." His appetite had been stolen by the words, Probability of paternity - 0%.

As Maddie gobbled up her oatmeal, he considered Doc's words. *Don't let a piece of paper define life for you. You get to choose, or at least your heart does.*

Layla wanted him to have Maddie, and until some man came knocking at his door to tell him Maddie was his, then she belonged to Alex. He had a birth certificate to prove it. Mercy was right, anyone could be a father, but it took a special man to be a daddy, and he wanted to be that man for Maddie.

"Hey, kiddo, are you ready to spend the day with Mercy?" He took a twenty from his wallet, set it on the table, and then tucked the envelope back into his pocket. What no one but he knew couldn't hurt anyone else, right?

CHAPTER FIFTEEN

Mercy hadn't seen Alex or Maddie for the past two days. He took Sunday and Monday off, and they headed to Denver to enjoy the zoo and museums.

Alex invited her to go with them, but she declined. A hotel room wasn't in her budget, and the alternative to sleeping with Alex, while tempting, wasn't right if Maddie was in the house, and they hadn't defined Alex and her relationship.

At this point, she was a babysitter that kissed him and let him feel her up a little. She didn't want to turn into the cliché nanny that slept with her boss to get a better life.

Her phone rang, and she answered it when Alex's name came up.

"Good morning."

"Back at ya."

His voice did things to her body. The deep timbre vibrated through her cells to sit in her core and throb.

"Are you on your way?" She shuffled through her unpaid bills and decided which one would get love this week.

"Yes, but I wanted to ask if you would join us for dinner. You're always cooking for us, but I thought I'd cook for you."

If her heart wasn't in this game already, it was now. "You want to cook for me?"

"I do. We want to spend more time with you because Mads missed you, and I did too."

They missed her. "I don't know," she teased. "I mean it's Aspen Cove and the center of all that's entertaining in the world. I thought about standing in my garden and waiting for a weed to sprout."

"Ooh." He whistled. "I don't know if I can beat that. All I can offer is a barbecued burger and me."

"Are you the appetizer or the dessert?" She loved the bantering between them. It was night and day from their first meeting when he accused her of leaving underwear, which she did, and she chastised him for treating Maddie like an inconvenience, which he had.

"I can be both."

"Hmm, when did you say Maddie had a sleepover?"

"Are you saying that you'd stay the night if I arranged one?"

She giggled. "All I'm saying is I like appetizers and dessert."

"See you in a few minutes." The phone was muffled when he told Maddie to get her bear, but when he uncovered it, he said. "I'll give you a sneak peek of what's to come when I get there."

As soon as they hung up, she raced to the bathroom to slick on some gloss and pink her cheeks. Looking into the mirror, she noticed a drop of coffee on her shirt, and there was no way she'd look like a slob when he came, so she rushed to her room to pick something else to wear.

It was supposed to be nearly eighty degrees today. That was hot for the mountains, but it was summer. When a search through her closet turned up nothing, she rummaged through her drawers. Since her legs were one of her finer features and Alex hadn't seen much of her, she chose shorts. Not the cargo ones that came to her knees, but the daisy dukes that barely covered her butt cheeks. She called them her gardening shorts since they didn't leave a funky tan line halfway down her thigh.

Dressed and back in the kitchen, she whipped up lunch for Alex. He often complained about having nothing but Dalton's take and bake pizza, and since she grilled chicken yesterday, she imagined a grilled chicken sandwich on a roll might be a nice change for him.

She had it all bagged when she heard them at the door. She hurriedly wrote, *Have a nice day*, and put a smiley face on a Post-it note and tucked it inside before she bustled to the door and swung it open.

Maddie rushed in and flung herself into Mercy's arms. "I missed you."

Mercy kissed the top of her head and squeezed her. "I missed you too." She also missed the heat in Alex's eyes, the same fiery passion she saw now when she glanced at him. "How was the zoo?"

"It was great, but there was this one lonely ape who would have loved to see a beautiful blonde with long legs visit."

"Is that so?" She turned Maddie around, so she faced the kitchen. "I made sugar cookies shaped like animals. Go pick one out while I talk to your dad." Maddie dashed to the kitchen, leaving them alone. Thankfully, kids were easy to distract.

Alex moved close enough for their chests to touch. "What did you want to talk to me about?"

"I thought you might like to tell me how much you missed me."

"Is there anything she can get into trouble with in there?" He nodded toward the kitchen.

"A stomachache if she eats too many cookies, but there's nothing on the stove, and the knives are put away. Why?"

He gripped her hips and lifted her. "Rather than tell you how much I missed you, I'll show you."

She wrapped her legs around his waist as he moved down the hallway and darted into the first open door. It was a spare room, the one Maddie took a nap in when she got tired.

Once inside, he kicked the door shut and pressed her against the wall before covering her mouth in a blistering kiss. His hand moved to her thighs, and he hoisted her higher on his waist but never stopped the kiss.

With her hand wrapped around his neck, she held on as if her life depended on it.

How could a kiss taste better than a sugar cookie? Was it that his cologne mixed with his pheromones threaded inside her brain to make her senseless?

When he pulled back, and their lips parted, she felt the loss of him.

"You must have only missed me a little if you quit the kiss so soon."

She slid down his body until her feet hit the ground. "That was only a taste," he said. "It was intended to whet your appetite for later."

She was wet, all right. "I'm definitely interested in more."

He ran his hands up her sides until they rested on her shoulders. "Glad to hear that." When he kissed the top of her head, he pulled back. "Would you mind bringing Maddie with you? I'll meet you at my house at around six."

"Six sounds great."

He leaned in for another kiss; only this one was long and languid and made her knees turn to liquid.

"I have to go. We're wrapping up the album this week. The faster I get there, the quicker I'll be home to make you dinner."

"Go then."

He opened the door and offered her his hand. When she clasped it, he brought the backside to his lips. "You're way too good for me."

"You're probably right, but my mom thinks I should take a walk on the wild side."

They walked hand in hand into the kitchen, where they found Maddie drawing in Mercy's notebook.

"Hey, Mads, Daddy's got to go to work," he said. "I'll see you for dinner. Mercy is coming over to eat."

The way Maddie was clapping and squealing you would have thought he'd told her he bought a pony.

Alex kissed Maddie on the head and brushed his lips across Mercy's.

"Daddy kissed you too."

Alex shook his head. "Kids don't miss a thing." He tugged Mercy to his side. "I like to kiss both of my girls." He leaned in and whispered. "Bring an appetite."

"Speaking of an appetite, I made you lunch to avoid another day of pizza."

His eyes softened. "You made me lunch?"

"Yes, it's a grilled chicken sandwich, chips, and a couple of cookies."

She opened the refrigerator and took out the bag to hand to him.

He held it to his chest. "I don't think I've ever had a woman make me a lunch."

"Not even your mom?"

He dropped his head. "No, she could barely make it out of bed most days."

She touched his arm. "You deserved better."

"Yep, but I got what I got." He glanced at Maddie, and Mercy swore she saw determination in his expression and knew in her heart he'd do better for his daughter.

As soon as Alex left, the usually quiet Maddie talked for over an hour about the weekend trip she had with her father. She told her about every animal she remembered in the zoo and how the museum had a big dinosaur in the first room they entered.

Though Mercy missed them, she was happy they had that time to bond. For someone so against being a father, Alex was turning out to be a darn good one. Maybe it was because he didn't have a choice. A child showed up, and she was his, and it wasn't as if he could return her.

The day passed quickly between Maddie's stories, their work in the garden, and a trip to the park. As it neared six o'clock, she considered changing her clothes, but he liked the shorts, and pleasing Alex was all she wanted to do today.

She heaved a sigh. Hadn't that been her problem in the past? She was always the pleaser and rarely the pleased. Then again, that kiss spoke to his ability to more than please her. If a single smooch could curl her toes and make her insides quiver, what else was Alex capable of?

"Are you ready to go home?" she asked Maddie.

"Can I have one more cookie? I didn't eat a wion, yet."

"No more cookies, but I'll save you a lion if you continue to practice your *L* sounds." She demonstrated once again by placing her tongue to the edge of her upper front teeth and said la la love, la la lion.

Old habits were hard to break, and because most people thought it was cute when small children mispronounced words like wuv for love, there was no incentive to correct the habit, but if a cookie would help, Mercy was happy to bake them.

Deciding to walk, they practiced the two sounds

Maddie had the most trouble with—Ls and Rs. By the time they turned onto Rose Lane, she could say them both with more clarity, but it would take time to make it a habit. That would be something to tackle another day.

Mercy scanned his fence for scraps of lingerie but found none. The door swung open, and Alex walked out holding the hand of a scantily clad brunette.

"Please let me stay," she said. "You know how good I can make you feel."

Mercy stopped and stared.

"Oh," Maddie said with a sigh. "Her again."

The words jolted Mercy back a step. "You know her?"

Maddie nodded. "She was in Daddy's bed last night."

Mercy's heart shattered because Alex was a liar. He said he missed her, but how could he when a bombshell brunette warmed his bed the night before.

Men were all the same. The whole lot of them were man whores. She wanted to turn and run, but she refused to leave Maddie on the sidewalk while the woman tried to climb Alex like a tree.

When he noticed her standing there, his eyes grew wide. "You're early."

She swallowed the lump in her throat. "We

walked because it's so nice out. Maybe I should have called first."

He peeled the woman off him. "It's not what it looks like."

The brunette stood back and stared at Mercy. "I only need like ten minutes. You can have him next."

"What?"

Alex pried himself away. "Stop it. That's my daughter over there."

It didn't slip past Mercy that he didn't explain who she was. What was she? Round two?

"I've got to go. Do you have Maddie?"

He broke loose, and when he rushed to her, the woman bolted back into his house.

"Mercy, please don't leave. You don't understand."

"Oh, I do. Don't forget, I've been in this exact situation before, always second choice."

She pivoted and started toward home.

CHAPTER SIXTEEN

"Stop."

Mercy's heart told her to do as he said, but her brain screamed for her to keep going. But being a woman ruled by her heart, she stopped and spun around to face him. "Look, Alex, I shouldn't be upset because we never defined what we were to each other, but for once, dammit, I'd like to be at the top of someone's list."

Flashing lights grabbed her attention, and the police cruiser stopped in front of the house.

Merrick jumped out. "Where is she?"

Alex nodded toward the house. "She probably locked herself inside." He tossed his keys to the deputy. "You'll need them."

"Stay here, and I'll take care of it."

Alex let out a breath. "Outside of posting a guard, what can I do to keep these women away?"

Mercy cocked her head, eyeing him. Did he say he wanted to keep those women away?

Alex turned to her. "You and I need to talk. If we're going to be together, then you have to trust me."

She'd been burned by giving her love freely and completely, did she have it in her to trust again?

Merrick entered the door, and within minutes, he had a kicking and screaming woman cuffed and in the back of his car. "Since this is the second time in two days, do you want to press charges?" Merrick looked over his shoulder to the cruiser. "I know you tried to be nice by giving her a warning last night, but see what that got you?"

"I hate to give her a criminal record for being a fan."

"She already has one for stalking someone else. She's not a fan, she's a fanatic."

Mercy listened to the exchange. She had it all wrong.

"Now that I have a daughter and a girlfriend," he turned to Mercy and lifted a brow and waited like he expected her to argue, "I can't have random women sneaking into my house, so yes, I think it's time I pressed charges."

"You got it," Merrick said before he climbed in the cruiser and drove away.

Mercy was sure she'd heard him wrong when he said she was his girlfriend. When did that happen? Was it their first kiss or the last one?

"Your what?"

Alex moved close enough for her to feel the heat come off his body.

"Come inside, and I'll explain."

What did she have to lose? "I imagine once we're inside, I'll owe you an apology?"

He slung his arm over Mercy's shoulder. "That would be a good place to begin." He walked them to Maddie and ruffled her hair. "Come on, kiddo, it's time to go in."

Once inside, he led them into the kitchen, where two grocery bags sat on the counter.

"Can I go play?" Maddie asked.

Alex nodded. "I'll be right back; I want to check the house and make sure everything is in order."

"Can I do anything to help?"

"Open a beer or pour a glass of wine and enjoy. I'll take it from here." He reached into the bag and pulled out both options before he walked away with Maddie on his heels.

Since Alex didn't drink, this was for her benefit. She chose the beer and tucked the bottle of wine in his refrigerator. She didn't care if it was red, white, or rose, she liked her wine cold.

Inside were shelves filled with fruits and vegetables and little yogurts in child size packages. There were bags of pre-sliced apples, cheese sticks, and a protein pack with cheese bits and nuts mixed with cranberries.

This was a refrigerator filled with love.

When he returned, he moved in front of her.

"Mercy, even though I haven't been in a monogamous relationship, I'd never cheat."

She picked up her beer and took a drink, all the while looking at him like he'd grown a third eye. "Do you realize how ridiculous that sounded." It wasn't her intention to be mean, even though it came out sounding that way. "How would a man who has never been monogamous know if he'd cheat?"

He set his hands on her shoulders. "Because when I'm with you, I don't want to be with anyone else."

"That sounds fine and dandy, but what happens when you're not with me? What about when you're on the road, and some hot brunette only needs you for ten minutes?"

He brushed his thumb over her lips before tilting her head up. "Let's flip the script for a minute. Do you think I want someone whose only desire is to have me for ten minutes? Frankly, that's an insult on many levels. Ten minutes? Really? What I have to offer takes a lot longer than that."

"You're offended that she wanted you?" Her neck ached from staring up at him, but there was no way she'd look anywhere else. Staring into his eyes, she saw the things he didn't say. Things like he was vulnerable and maybe a little scared.

"No, it's nice that someone finds me attractive, but at some point, I have to ask, is there something deeper?" He chuckled. "She told me I looked like her father, but she'd do me anyway."

"Seriously?"

"Apparently, my haircut aged me."

She lifted her hand to his head and raked her fingers through the soft strands. "I like it better than the long stuff."

He leaned into her touch. "Me too. It's cooler and easier to care for."

"She's crazy, but if you look like her father, then he's one sexy man."

"Sexy, huh?"

She never considered a rock star could be insecure when they had everything they wanted from money to women. "Does your ego need stroking?"

He bent toward her, brushed his lips against hers, and whispered, "That and other things."

Her curiosity peaked. "What other things?" she teased.

"How about we eat and figure it out together?"

"Together sounds good."

Side by side, they worked together, making dinner. He hadn't wanted her help, but she figured the quicker they got to dinner, the faster they'd get to *dessert*.

Just as the burgers finished grilling, Maddie walked out, carrying her backpack.

"Where are you going?" Mercy asked.

"I have a sleepover with Ms. Louise."

Not only had the idea of a sleepover thrown her, but Maddie pronounced her Ls. She swooped down and picked her up for a hug.

"I'm so proud of you. I loved that you said, Louise."

Maddie hugged Mercy's neck tightly, and with her mouth at her ear, she whispered. "I wuv you."

Even though she didn't get the *L* right, those three words made Mercy's heart full. Maddie had come to her at a time when she needed something to brighten her day. She never thought it would be a five-year-old who'd steal her heart. Then again, she had one good-looking father.

"I love you, too." She set her down, and when she stood, Alex's eyes seemed glassy.

He turned away and flipped the burgers one last time. "You know, for some, love comes easy, but for people like me—people who have lost so much so early, love is risky. Why would I give my heart to another person who would likely destroy it?"

Was that a warning or a confession for why he whored around?

"I get it completely. It's the once burned, twice shy thing."

He plated the burgers and set them on the outside table where they'd put the fixin's and the buns.

"Yes, I imagine you get it. And you're right. My statement about monogamy was ridiculous, but my point was that even though I'd never tried it, once I was in a relationship, I'd be faithful. I can't expect there to be different rules for us."

She helped Maddie with her burger and gave her a handful of chips.

"Are we in a relationship?" Was it possible to let go of the past and move on? Everyone else seemed to do it, so why not her?

"I would like to think that we are." He doctored his burger. "I arranged for that sleepover we talked about but given the lead up to tonight's dinner, maybe it's best if we wait. I don't want you to feel obligated in any way to stay."

She looked at Maddie, who had ketchup on her cheeks. "Are you excited about your sleepover?"

Maddie swallowed and grinned. "They have Barbies."

"So easy to please," Alex said. He laid his hand on

top of Mercy's. "I'm sorry about earlier. I didn't invite her. I swear some of these women are like mice and can find their way inside the tiniest openings."

"Your cameras didn't catch her?"

"It would seem I have a blind spot. I ordered a few more Arlo cameras and will install them as soon as they arrive." He squeezed her hand.

"I'm sorry too. I jumped to conclusions, and I'm ashamed of myself."

Alex looked at Maddie. "Hey, Mads, is it okay if I kiss Mercy?"

Maddie giggled. "Yuck."

"Just keep thinking that until you're about thirty-five."

Alex leaned in and gave Mercy a sweet kiss that left her wanting more.

They finished their burgers and cleaned up but stayed outside where the night air was cool.

Alex's backyard was nothing to write home about. It had grass, and that was it. Maddie chased a butterfly with nowhere to land because his yard, like his house, was stark.

"You should plant a garden," she said. "Maddie loves to help."

He scooted his seat closer, so they sat side by side. "I wouldn't know where to begin."

"I could help too. It's too late to plant fruits and vegetables, but we can prep it for next year." She pointed to the right corner. "You could put a cutting garden right there where it gets full sun and have fresh flowers all summer long. That corner," she nodded to the left, "would be perfect for berries, and along the back, I can see rows of carrots and radishes and maybe a few giant sunflowers."

He intertwined his fingers with hers. "Is that what you want?"

"I have a garden already. It has to be what you want because gardens are a lot like kids: they take commitment and care."

"All I want is for you to spend the night so I can show you that I'm capable of commitment and care."

"Who has to make breakfast in the morning?"

"We'll go to Maisey's."

"Deal." Holy hell, she just agreed to spend the night with Alex Cruz. By morning, she'd know all about his wooden stick.

———

THEY STOOD at the door and waved goodbye to Maddie.

"I've been thrown over for a Barbie Dreamhouse and Ken." Alex shut the door and led Mercy into the living room.

"A daughter's first love is always her father."

He sat first and tugged her onto his lap. "Was that your first love?"

"Yes, until Timmy Bloom brought me a bag of Skittles, and then I was his until he tossed me aside for Kathy Stevens because she was cheap and easy. She kissed him behind the slide."

When he rubbed his hand up her leg, she prayed she didn't have stubble.

"Men think they want cheap and easy, but that usually turns into expensive and complicated. I'm finding out it's the ones you wait for that mean the most."

She glanced at his hand, where his fingers had slipped under the edge of her shorts.

"Is that what you call waiting?"

"For me? Anything past five minutes is a lifetime."

"What if I would have said no to the sleepover?"

He lifted his hand and touched her cheek. "I would have waited." He let his head fall back against the leather couch. "I've been doing life my way for years, and it seemed to be fine, but then a woman and a girl were thrust into my existence, and everything changed. I didn't know what I needed until I realized how much I lived without."

She leaned her head on his shoulder. "But you hated me the first day we met."

"Hate is a strong word. I thought you were like the rest and out to get what you could from me."

She considered him and his life, and it made her sad. "You and I aren't much different." Her shoulders shook with laughter. "I mean, we are totally different, but the people in our lives have used us. The only difference between us is that I had good role models, and I should have known better. But you, by the sounds of it, couldn't have known."

"It's easy to blame ignorance. I watched my mom die from loneliness while my father lived happily with his fame and women. His life seemed far more pleasurable, so I modeled mine after his. But now that I have Maddie, I'm scared to death. I need to do better. I know how I've been as a man, and I wouldn't want my daughter to date someone like me."

She sat up and studied him. "But you want me to date you?"

"I do because, when I'm with you, I'm a better person." He lifted to reach her lips and talk about their past ended. With his mouth on hers, there was nothing left to consider but the tingle and pulsing in her core.

Desire hit her, hard and fast. Shifting so she straddled him, she ran her hands up and down his chest. Every muscle rippled under her touch. "Take this off."

"My girl is demanding." He pushed back into the

couch and reached between them to pull off his shirt.

Lord almighty, the man was made of stone. She let her fingers trail across his bare chest.

"Your turn." She had no time to consider his words before he had the hem of her top moving past her chin. When it was free, he tossed it aside to land on top of his shirt.

His eyes focused on her breasts. They probably weren't like the ones he was used to. Hers were real.

He pulled the lace down to reveal nipples that seemed to reach for his mouth. And when his lips touched them, she closed her eyes and moaned. Full lips and hot tongue alternated between suckling and sucking. He made her want things she wasn't sure were possible, like love and multiple Os.

Grinding against him, he hardened to steel beneath her—his thickness fitting perfectly between her thighs.

He shifted and stood with her in his arms. Long-legged and quick on his feet, he had them in his room in seconds.

"Was she in your bed?" She hated to ruin the moment, but when they made love, she wanted to be the only woman to have touched those sheets.

"No, she was on the comforter, which I tossed in the wash already."

She glanced at the bed to see it covered with a thin blanket.

"Carry on, then."

He set her down and went straight for the button of her shorts. It didn't take him long to get her fully naked.

She lifted on her elbows. "Your turn."

God was he sexy with a lift to his brow and a smirk on his face. Shirtless, he tugged the button on his jeans loose and pulled the zipper down one tooth at a time. For a man who was in such a hurry moments ago, he wasn't rushing now. He took his time undressing, and she loved the suspense. Having her attention focused on him made her forget all the ways she might be inadequate—almost.

"Hey, what just happened? It looked like I lost you." He stopped stripping and climbed onto the bed with her. "I saw something change in your eyes. If this isn't what you want, we can wait."

She rolled to her side to face him. "I don't want to wait, but I don't want to disappoint you either. We've got something special building that I don't want to ruin it with bad sex."

His eyes widened. "Seriously? You think there's any possibility that I won't enjoy what we're about to do?"

She bit her lower lip and nodded.

He took her hand and held it against his denim-covered length. "Does this feel like I'm not enjoying you?"

"No."

"Then let's get out of your head and into us. Only we belong in this bed. You didn't want the groupie here, and I don't want your ex. He was an idiot. A lesser man would have already finished in the living room when you were grinding on me. That was so hot." He slid his hand over her body and settled his palm over her breast. "These are perfect." He gently pinched her nipple, pulling a moan from her. "That response is everything." He moved his hand down her stomach until it rested on her mound. "This is a freaking playground for a man who knows how to use the equipment." His mouth followed the trail of his hand until he settled his shoulders between her thighs and let his tongue loose.

Her body was a tightrope and her nerves the acrobat teetering and tottering on the edge. Every few seconds, she was certain she would fall forward and float blissfully back to earth, but she was tethered to Alex, and he kept her body ready to fly.

Shuddering beneath him, she could no longer avoid the fall and tumbled fiercely, spinning, gasping, pulsing until she lay on the bed spent and panting.

Alex was there to catch her.

When their eyes connected, all she saw was a

predator who had gotten his first taste. She was a mouse who'd entered the lion's den.

"Did you like that?"

What was not to like? "I now know why women are sneaking into your house."

"Not for that. That's far too intimate for a stranger."

Could a heart break from happiness? Was hers too full to hold the joy he'd given her? "Really?"

He moved next to her and covered her mouth with his. She was on his lips, in his mouth, and hopefully protected somewhere in his heart.

After a long kiss, he stood and dropped his pants. That hungry look in his eyes grew fiercer. "What do you like, Mercy?"

She had no idea. She certainly liked what she'd experienced so far. "Do you have a menu?"

He pulled a condom from the nightstand drawer and rolled it on. "Do you want me to make one?"

She reached and tugged him on top of her—his heavy length pressing between her legs.

"No, I'm feeling a bit greedy tonight. How about you give me all that you got?"

And in one swift thrust, he did. He filled her in places she didn't know existed. It wasn't just body to body; they were soul to soul. If this was how the night started, she was sure there would be no sleep in their sleepover.

CHAPTER SEVENTEEN

Alex called Louise to let her know he'd pick Maddie up and take her to breakfast.

"Did you two have a nice night?" Louise asked.

Nice didn't begin to describe what the evening was like. He had plenty of marathon nights in his past, but none left him feeling like he wanted more. His life was changing faster than his brain could process.

"Thanks for watching Maddie."

Louise laughed. "I like a man who doesn't kiss and tell. Not sure how hungry Maddie will be since the kids polished off two cereal boxes, but she'll be happy to see you."

"Did she do okay?"

"Something tells me Maddie's done a lot of sleep-overs somewhere else."

He knew it was true in the back of his mind, but it unsettled him to think that she'd been carted around and slept in strange places so her mom could get a fix or check off another bucket list person.

"I'm sure you're right. Again, thank you."

"Anytime. We loved having her."

Hands slipped around his waist from behind, and a glorious set of lips kissed his bare back.

"We've got thirty minutes to shower and get Maddie."

She moved in front of him, and God did she look sexy wearing his shirt. Seeing her in his clothes was almost as good as seeing her wearing him.

"A shower will only take fifteen minutes." She gave him that look that said she was ready for more.

He lifted her up until she wrapped her legs around his waist. "You are my kind of woman."

She leaned in and whispered. "Ready and willing?"

"No, although I like that you are, you're so much more than that."

"Tell me."

"Lord, have mercy on me."

"You've got about fourteen minutes to make that happen."

He moved to the bedroom in a flash.

THEY WERE five minutes late picking up Maddie, but she didn't seem to mind. When she noticed them at the door, she ran with open arms and went straight to Mercy. At first, it pricked at his heart, but one look at the two of them hugging, and he was sure if the tables turned, he would have run to Mercy too.

"Are you hungry?"

Maddie looked at him. "Can I have a pancake with chocolate chips?" She pronounced the L carefully as if making sure she got it right.

"You can have anything you want."

"Then, I'm hungry."

He took her from Mercy and hoisted her to his hip, then turned back to Louise.

"Thank you. I can't tell you how much I appreciate you watching Mads."

Louise waved him off. "It wasn't anything we wouldn't do for another Aspen Cove family member."

Was this what family was like? "I'm a little rusty on the family thing. I've never had one."

She touched his arm. "They're a little like plants; you talk to them, water and feed them, and make sure they're taken care of. Some are prickly, and some are pretty and sweet. Some are downright poisonous, but they all have a place in our lives."

Between Doc and Louise and Mercy, he was being schooled. He used to think he had it all figured out until he came to Aspen Cove, and they taught him that he didn't know squat about anything.

When they got to the diner, he was starving and knew Mercy could eat a few blue-plate specials on her own with the calories she burned. Anyone that said he couldn't lose weight making love was crazy.

Maisey came by and took their order. With her glasses perched low on her nose, she studied the three of them.

"Looks to me like you've got a nice little family started here."

Alex looked at Mercy, whose jaw had dropped.

"It's not like that." Mercy blushed. "I work for Alex, and we're friends."

If she'd picked up her knife and stabbed him, it would have hurt less. Hadn't last night proved they were more than friends? He'd never let a woman spend the night because that was far too risky. His father had warned him early on that if they stayed the night, they remained too long. Then again, his father was an asshole.

"Hmm," Maisey hummed and looked straight at Mercy. "I learned long ago to stop lying to myself." She tapped her back end. "I'll never lose that last twenty pounds, and no matter what products I use, I'll never have the skin of a twenty-year-old, but the biggest lie I used to tell myself was that I didn't need love because I could love myself and that was enough." She glanced over her shoulder to see Ben sliding an order across the pickup window. "That man there proved I was wrong."

She waited with her order pad and pen.

Alex paused for Mercy to order, but he ordered for all three of them when she didn't. "Two blue-plate specials and a chocolate chip pancake." He winked at Maddie. "Extra chocolate, please."

She bounced in her seat. "Thank you, Daddy, I w ... love you."

He reached across the table to tap her button nose. "I love you too, squirt."

"See, love is special. You can't buy it, and you can't make it, it just is. When it's right, it's incredible." Maisey turned and walked away.

"What did last night mean to you?" he asked once Maisey was gone.

She studied him for a moment. "Everything."

Had he been holding his breath? When she confirmed that it was something special, a whoosh left his lungs.

"To me too." He didn't know what happened to the Alex who arrived in town. The man with the long hair and rock star attitude. Somehow, he disappeared, and the man he was becoming took his place.

They finished their breakfast to the chatter of

Maddie talking about Barbies and some kind of talking doll.

"We're going to stop at the bookstore first, so Maddie and I can walk home from there."

He paid the bill and left. Once outside, he kissed Maddie on the head and Mercy on the lips.

"I'll see you for dinner. How about I bring a pizza from Dalton's?"

Maddie didn't waste any time with her yes, and seeing how excited she was, Mercy seemed to acquiesce.

"I thought you were tired of pizza."

"I'm willing to sacrifice for the women in my life."

"Pizza it is, then." She turned toward the bookstore while he climbed into his SUV and headed for the studio.

Gray was the only one there when he arrived.

"How's that cute little teacher? Are you banging her yet?"

Alex's first reaction was to put a fist in Gray's face, but that would make for an awkward work environment. It was already tense between Deanna and Red. Indigo didn't need another conflict happening. That's how bands split up. Somehow it was always over egos and women.

"Hey, man, don't talk about Mercy that way."

Gray's brows lifted. "Holy shit. You are banging her."

Alex's hands fisted at his side. He walked to his drums to put distance between them.

"She's special."

"Dude, you're such a cliché. Single dad doing it with the nanny."

He took a threatening step forward. "I'm asking nicely that you don't talk about Mercy like she's some groupie. I like her. More than like her. She's good for Maddie and me. Hell, she might be the one."

Gray held up his hands like he surrendered. "You're thinking with the wrong head. When it comes to women, the head on your shoulders shouldn't be ruling your world. I'm not saying you can't appreciate her or treat her right, but you know it never works out. Think about all the shit you'll go through. The jealousy alone is a killer, and then you have to choose between your career and her. Women murder your dreams, man. I should know, I was married once, and still paying for that experience."

Alex grabbed his drum key and tuned his set while waiting for the rest of the band to arrive.

During their session, he considered all the ways Gray could be right and wrong.

Jealousy would always be an issue, but that's where trust came in. When the day ended, rather than hang out and chat with his bandmates, he rushed to Mercy's with a fresh pizza.

He found his girls in the backyard picking strawberries, and by the mess on Maddie's face, more ended up in her mouth than in the basket.

"Hey," Mercy rose from her knees and walked straight to him, offering him a kiss.

"I hope you don't mind that I walked in. You didn't come when I knocked, and the door was unlocked."

She brushed her hands off on her denim shorts before she set them on his chest. "You can come in anytime you want." She lifted on tiptoes and kissed him slowly and thoroughly. If this was what coming home was going to be like, he wanted more.

There was a tug on his belt loop. "Hello, Daddy."

"Hey, squirt." Each time she called him Daddy, it melted his heart. He was so wrong to dismiss her initially. His past behavior put him at risk for fathering many children. While he always used a condom, he didn't think about the failure rate.

Then the rage set in. Maddie wasn't even his, but he cared about her and for her. He had an opportunity to make her life better.

"There's pizza in the kitchen."

When Maddie ran off, he tugged Mercy closer to him. "I missed you."

"I missed you too." She laid her head against his chest and inhaled. "You always smell good."

"I shower."

The sound of her laughter was as sweet as music. "I know. That was the second-best part of my day."

"And the first?"

"Before the shower."

"We'll need to arrange for another sleepover soon."

She stepped back and threaded her arm through his, and they walked into the house where Maddie already had the pizza box open. She held a slice in one hand and a pen in the other.

Mercy opened the refrigerator and took out a pitcher of sweet tea.

Maddie tore off a sheet of paper from the pad and handed it to him. On the front were three stick figures that he imagined were Maddie, Mercy, and him. When he turned it over to see what was on the back, his stomach dropped into his shoes.

At the top of the sheet was the words Bucket List, and below in the number one position was groupie underlined.

"Was that all this was?" He held up the list and stared at Mercy, who took the seat across from him. "Am I just a bucket list item to be checked off?" He glanced at the bottom and took Maddie's pen. "Here, you might as well scratch earth-shattering Os from the list." He drew a line through the entry.

"Oh, come on, Alex. That's not what this is." She swiped the page and tossed it away, then handed Maddie a fresh sheet and a new pen. "Honey, can you draw your father another picture?"

"Finish eating, Maddie, because we need to go home."

Maddie scowled at him. "But I'm drawing."

"I know, sweetie, but Daddy has stuff to do."

"Alex, that sheet is BS, and the only reason groupie was at the top was because my mom told me to become one just once."

"You succeeded and didn't even have to break in; I invited you. Sorry I can't help with number three because I've already got one child, and I'm not looking for another."

"Stop." She reached for his hand, but he yanked it away. "Let's talk in the other room." She eyed Maddie and nodded toward the living room.

He followed her. "Stop?" He attempted to keep his voice low, but he was a hair away from yelling. "You're just like the rest. Let's land a night with the drummer and see if he's good with his stick."

She faced him and fisted her hips. If he weren't so crushed, he'd think she was cute with her defiant stance. "You know, if we're going to have a relation-ship, you have to trust me."

"Relationship?" He cleared his throat. "I don't have much experience with them, but I'm fairly certain they don't start with a bucket list where the first entry is a groupie, and the last is earth-shattering Os."

She stalked forward and poked his chest. If she were a man, she'd be laid out on the ground, but he'd never hit a woman.

"I'm not a groupie."

"Is that why you shoved your underwear in my fence?"

She rolled her eyes. "Okay, I went over to your house to do a groupie thing, but that was the extent. And I chose your house as opposed to the others because you're not my type."

His insides twisted like his intestines were wrapped with rusty wire. "I was sure your type last night."

She let out a muffled scream. "Oh, my God. Listen to me. You had long hair, which is not my thing. Your house seemed to be a fan favorite, so I figured I could rush in and rush out without getting caught. Then I met you, and everything changed. You were a complete asshole, but a hot asshole. When you brought Maddie because you needed me ... well, all I can say is every day since then I've fallen for you. And last night ... that was the most amazing experience of my life. Believe me, or don't believe me, but it's the truth." She put her palms together like a prayer. "I hope you believe me because I can't imagine my life without you now that I've had you."

Every word sounded sincere. How could he argue with what she said? Everyone does stupid, silly stuff. "You didn't like my long hair?" He opened his arms, and she fell into them. "I'm sorry. I shouldn't have jumped to conclusions."

"No more groupies for either of us, okay?" she asked.

"How about you be my one and only groupie?" He squeezed her tightly, never wanting to let her go.

"That's a deal."

Maddie walked out of the kitchen with a new picture. Her stick figure father held her hand, and on her other side was a woman, but in the sky was another.

"Who's this?" He pointed to the stick figure with the long hair holding her other hand.

"That's Mercy." Her pizza-sauce-dirtied finger pointed to the sky where a woman floated. "That's Mommy, and she's happy I'm here."

CHAPTER EIGHTEEN

It had been three days since they argued—three days of kisses and stolen moments.

An hour ago, Katie invited Maddie over on the pretense that her daughter Sahara needed a play date.

When Mercy texted Alex that Maddie was playing at Katie's and she was home alone, he said he'd be there in minutes.

She had no idea what he would tell the band, but it made her feel important that he dropped everything for her. Not once in her adult life had anyone put her first, and the feeling was addictive.

Waiting, she sat at the table and wrote several checks to bill collectors. The eight hundred dollars a week she charged Alex was a boon and a bane. She needed the money desperately, but guilt ate at her for charging him so much. Then again, when they negotiated the price, she wasn't in love with him. That scary feeling of want and need and desire crawled into her heart and curled up all cozy and warm. Was what she felt for Alex, love? She couldn't figure out any other emotion that made her feel this good.

A soft tap sounded at the door, and her blood rushed through her veins, heating her body. Alex was here for her.

Her heart hadn't beat this hard since her wedding day, and in all honesty, that wasn't excitement, but anxiousness that had it doing double time. There was no wedding dress, no veil, no wedding party. She stood in a courtroom in front of a judge, because it was financially practical, but it seemed as though it was more of a punishment than a joyous occasion, almost like she signed up for a life sentence without a chance of parole, or so she thought.

When she opened the door, she found Mr. Sexy leaning on the doorframe.

"Delivery for Ms. Mercy."

"Did I order something?"

"You did, and I'm here to deliver."

She stood aside and let him enter. If her grin got any wider, her face might split. "I like my deliveries hot."

He pushed the door shut and reached for the hem of his shirt, pulling it up and over his head.

Holy hell, he was a work of art.

"You make me burn inside, but only you can judge whether or not I'm hot." He stalked toward her. "Now, you, on the other hand, are sizzling." He walked her back until she hit the wall. " What's hot is standing right here, pushing you against the drywall and kissing you like I never want to stop."

"Oh, God," she said on a shaky exhale. "Kiss me then."

His mouth covered hers, and he made a sound like the purr of a contented cat.

She loved the way he didn't rush anything. The one thing about Alex was he was all in and totally present.

He savored her kisses like they were special. A brush against her lips. A bite that stung, but quickly relieved when he sucked her lip into his mouth and soothed it with a swipe of his tongue.

Every nerve ending came alive and tingled like energy skirting over her skin. It was like the feeling of electricity hitting ground so close that it made the hairs on her arms stand.

"Take this off." He tugged at her shirt until it was free and tossed it to land near his.

"How much time do we have?" she panted.

He tugged at the button on his jeans. "When do

you have to get Maddie?" Alex always went commando, so when his jeans dropped, and he kicked off his shoes, he was gloriously naked.

"Forty minutes."

"How late do you think you can be? Forty-minutes is not enough."

Bubbly laughter burst forth. It was the same happy sound she made when she opened a present.

"I don't think she'll hold me to the minute."

"I like this town more and more." He tugged her jeans free, and once the condom was on, he pressed inside her. For the next hour, Alex made love to her all over the house.

She would never be able to walk around her home and not see him in every corner—feel him in her muscle memory.

When they finished, he gave her another passionate kiss. The kind that said he'd be back.

"YOU'RE GLOWING," Katie said. "I guess you had a playdate too?"

They sat at Katie's kitchen table, sipping sweet tea, and staring at the calm lake. A passing boat sent a ripple across the glassy surface. Alex was her ripple.

"It was a pleasant hour."

"You could have taken two." She looked over her

shoulder, where the girls sat side by side on the sofa, holding hands and watching Dora the Explorer. "Aren't they precious?"

A sad look flashed across Katie's face.

"Something wrong?" Mercy asked.

Katie heaved a sigh. "Not really. I mean, how could anything be wrong? I'm alive, I've got the best husband, and Sahara is my miracle child, but sometimes I wish I could have more. A brother or sister for my baby would have been nice." She tapped the space above her heart. "Bad ticker."

It wasn't hard to learn about residents in a small town, and Katie was a pink letter recipient of Bea's, a woman Mercy never met but would have loved to. Katie didn't only inherit the bakery, but she was also the recipient for Bea's daughter's heart when Brandy died. The tale was fascinating and something perfect for a Hallmark movie.

"I always wanted a houseful of children. Since I'll never have any of my own, I have to parent vicariously through other's children," Mercy said.

"I thought I'd risk it to give Bowie a son, but as soon as I mentioned it, he had a vasectomy. He wasn't willing to lose me."

"How did you know he was the one?"

She laid her palm over her chest. "I just knew. Bowie was actually quite the a-hole at first, but I softened his disposition. What about you? Is Alex the one?"

She waved the question away. "It hasn't been long enough to really know."

"Yes, it has. If there's something there, you know it."

She watched a water-skier zip past Katie's dock, leaving the water churning and lapping against the shore.

"My inner voice constantly warns me not to fall too soon because there's so much to lose when love goes wrong."

"You didn't have a good one the first time. Don't put yourself out to pasture because one bull was bad." Katie's Texas upbringing was always present in her accent, but her reference was straight from the Lone Star state, or at least it sounded authentically Texan to Mercy's untrained ears.

"In all fairness, it wasn't all Randy's fault. There is a lesson to be learned from being a pleaser. Maybe while I focused on being the best wife, cook, and housekeeper, I overlooked more important things. I thought he was madly in love with me until that knock on the door."

Katie silently shook her head. "That was on him and not you. Now back to Alex. What do you feel?"

"I'm falling fast and hard. Alex is everything I thought I'd loathe and yet it turns out I love it all."

She chuckled. "Not the groupies. They are my biggest concern. What happens when he's on the road, and women show up on the bus and his hotel room?"

Katie sat for a moment as if contemplating. "You have to trust him to do the right thing. No one can give him what you do."

"Not true. A million women are willing to try, and I'm sure they all have something good to offer."

Katie topped off their glasses of sweet tea. "Don't repeat your mistakes. In my experience, a man who has to work harder appreciates you more."

She had a point. She wasn't impressed with Alex when they met. He didn't win her over with his fame and fortune.

"I wasn't easy at first. We banged heads long before we banged bodies."

"You're already different from the rest. They wanted something from him, and you didn't."

She took a long drink and let the sweet liquid ease down her throat. "He pays me to watch Maddie."

"He should because she's not your daughter."

That truth cut her deep. "I wish she was. I don't know what her mom was like, but from the things she's said, and after listening to the friend tell Alex the cause of her demise, I can only imagine that she's seen enough sorrow to last a lifetime."

"Kids are resilient. Nothing about her screams

abused or neglected. You are a positive influence in her life, and that's another plus for you. How lucky was he to need a sitter just when you needed a job?"

"That was pretty remarkable—a much-needed coincidence."

Katie laughed and stared at the ceiling. "I think there's a higher power involved."

Mercy's brows lifted. "You mean, God?"

"No, I mean Bea. She's filled this town with pink letters and love, and I think she's up there working her magic on the people she never got a chance to meet."

"I like the thought of that. I could use a little heavenly interference in my life."

Maddie climbed off the couch and walked to stand in front of her. She tugged on the arm of Mercy's T-shirt. "Mommy, can we go home?"

Mercy stared at her. As she started to correct Maddie, Katie touched her arm. "I'm telling you, that's Bea at work, just go with it."

She'd have to talk with Maddie, so she didn't get confused, but today was not the time, so she pretended not to hear Mommy. "You ready, sweetheart?"

CHAPTER NINETEEN

Alex woke missing Mercy because moments with her were like eating potato chips—he couldn't have just one. Every time he was with her, he wanted more.

He poured a bowl of cereal for Maddie and made a cup of coffee for himself. Looking at the little girl in front of him, he considered how Aspen Cove had changed his life. The small town he reluctantly moved to brought him a world of frustration with obsessed fans, but it also brought him Maddie and Mercy and a whole cast of characters to color his life.

Maddie might not be his by blood, but she was his by choice.

"Daddy, when are we going to Mommy's?"

He stared at Maddie, confused. "Honey, we can't go see your mom." Hell, he didn't even know where to find her. Eventually, Maddie would want to visit her grave, and Alex would need to know where to find it. "She's in heaven."

"No, I mean, mommy Mercy."

He nearly dropped his coffee mug. "Why are you calling Mercy, mommy? Does she ask you to call her that?"

"No, but I want a mommy, and Ms. Mercy is a good one. She makes me cookies and lets me play in the sink. She rubs my back until I fall asleep when I'm tired. Mommy's should be nice, and she's nice."

He didn't want to mar the memory of Maddie's mother, but he needed more information.

"Was mommy Layla nice?"

Maddie shoved a spoonful of Cheerios in her mouth, and he waited for her to finish chewing and answer. All the while, her brows shifted, and her head tilted this way and that like she was pondering her answer.

"Yes, mommy was nice, but some of the daddies weren't. They yelled, and I don't like yelling."

A lump of sadness lodged in his throat and took two swallows of coffee to force it down. He knew what living in volatility was like. His mother was an emotional yo-yo. When his father was in town, which was rare, they'd have a day or two of a honeymoon phase, and then all hell broke loose.

His childhood was a vicious circle of loneliness,

drinking, yelling, and abandonment. Maybe that was why he was determined to give Maddie something better. In the beginning, it was because he didn't want to repeat his father's mistakes and abandon a child that belonged to him. But even after discovering that she wasn't biologically his kid, he knew deep inside she was exactly like him anyway. As the daughter of a groupie, she probably never knew stability. Who knew how many couches she slept on while Layla marked off boxes on her bucket list. How many men were on it?

He studied Maddie to see if he recognized anyone in her features, but when she looked up at him, all he saw was himself. How lucky was he that Layla gifted him with a child—a child he didn't know he wanted or needed until she showed up.

"I'm sorry, Mads. People get angry, and sometimes they yell. That's never fun." He took the seat next to her. "Were you scared?"

She nodded.

"Did anyone ever hurt you?"

She shrugged.

Rage rushed through him, pricking at his skin like angry bee stings. She was five for God's sake, and at five, her life should be filled with sandcastles and ice cream cones.

"No one will ever hurt you again." He made a mental note to take Maddie to Doc's to get a complete physical. She'd need one for school anyway. He hadn't considered a therapist but would talk to Doc about it the next time he saw him.

"Finish your cereal, and I'll comb your hair before we go to Mercy's." Just thinking about the pretty blonde made his body react. He remembered only a handful of times when he'd slept with a woman more than once. Layla was one of them because she was attractive, and if he were honest, a beast in bed, but no matter how much fun those moments were, the time he spent with Mercy was special. They connected on a deeper level.

Maddie finished her cereal and skipped to the bathroom to get the brush and whatever hair tie she chose. Today, Maddie was in a hurry to get to Mercy's, so a single ponytail with a green ribbon was all she wanted.

When it was done, she was out the door. All he'd given her was a place to live, safety, and love, and she bloomed like one of the mammoth sunflowers in Mercy's garden.

"Can you stay with us and go to the park?"

He buckled her into the booster and kissed her cheek. "I wish I could, but Daddy missed some practice yesterday, and he has to lay down his tracks for the album."

She stuck her bottom lip out in a pout, and he

wondered if that was a learned trait or if it came naturally.

"I'll make it up to you."

Before he could back out, she placed her hands on his cheeks and pulled him closer. "I love you, Daddy."

"Love you too, squirt."

He rounded the car and climbed inside. The drive to Mercy's only took minutes, but in that time, he counted all the blessings he had. There were ones he never knew he needed. While he didn't have the kind of childhood he wished for, he could do better for Maddie.

She was tugging on her seat belt when they pulled in front of Mercy's bungalow. As soon as he let her free, Maddie raced to where she was on the porch.

"Slow down, or you might fall." An *ugh* sound burst from Mercy when Maddie plowed into her.

"Mommy Mercy, I missed you."

Mercy froze. "Honey, I'm not your—"

"Hey," he broke in before she could finish the sentence.

She shuffled Maddie to the door and told her to sit in the reading chair, and she'd be there in a moment.

"I'm sorry," she said, as soon as they were alone. "I don't know where that came from. She said it yesterday at Katie's, too. Maybe she's missing her mom."

"I don't think so. Maybe she sees that you treat her better than her mother ever did."

"I don't want her to get confused. It's probably not wise to let her call me something like mommy. I mean, if things didn't work out, then I'd be another loss in her life."

He cocked his head. "Is something not working out between us?" He prowled toward her. "Yesterday, everything was perfect."

"Yes, but yesterday isn't forever."

He touched his lips softly to hers. "Every day is the first day of forever."

HE WAS HALFWAY through his set when his phone vibrated in his pocket, and he snuck out of the studio to answer it. They were busy listening to play-backs, so the timing was perfect.

"This is Alex."

"Hey man, it's Pablo."

What the hell was Pablo calling him for? The last time he'd seen him was at his father's memorial.

"What's up? Where have you been?"

"You know," there was a chuckle. "Living the dream." There was a moment of silence. "Did you hear that Drive Shaft is being inducted into the Rock Music Hall of Fame?"

"Yes, I saw that. Congrats." He read about it and knew his father would have laughed. Bastian Cruz never cared for the awards. He lived for the music.

"That's why I'm calling. Since your father isn't here, we thought you might want to sit in for him at the awards ceremony. I know it's last minute, but you're not an easy man to get ahold of."

"Should have asked a fan. They have no problems getting to me."

"What do you say? We also have a limited tour starting that week for a month, and we'd love for you to join us."

When he was a kid, he wanted to be just like his father. He dreamed of playing in the band and going on tour with his father's bunch of rowdies. Through a child's eyes, everything looked exciting and glamorous until birthdays and Christmas were forgotten, and phone calls never came.

Red walked out of the studio and leaned against the wall.

"Hey, Pablo, give me a minute." Alex put his hand over the phone. "Drive Shaft wants me to fill in for my father for the music awards and the following mini-tour."

"Holy shit."

"I know, but I've got Maddie."

Red lifted his brow. "Dude, you can't pass this up. It's a once in a lifetime deal. That was your dad's band. How many people can do that? Besides, you have Mercy, and I'm sure she'll understand and watch Maddie."

He was right. It was a gift. He brought the phone up to his ear. "I'm in. When do I have to be there?"

"As soon as you can. We need to get you up to date with your dad's guitar riffs."

"I'll try to get out there within a day or two."

"See ya soon, kid."

He hung up and rolled his eyes. No one had called him kid in years.

Red slapped him on the back. "Let's tell the group."

"Hopefully, we can find a fill-in for the concert." He hadn't considered the Fireman's Fundraiser, but knowing Samantha, she wouldn't want him to miss the opportunity.

When he went back inside, he got the blessings of the band; now, all he had to do was get Mercy's.

CHAPTER TWENTY

Mercy glanced at Maddie, who stood on a stool playing in a sink full of water. She was a curious little thing, and today's experiment was to see what would float.

Mercy believed that hands-on was the best way to learn, and she let Maddie try anything as long as she couldn't ruin it or get hurt. That was why her outside table was covered with things that didn't float like oven mitts and shoes so they could dry.

"Hey, Mads ... should we make that banana pudding your dad likes so much?"

"Yes." Maddie clapped her sudsy hands, wiped the moisture on her shorts, and jumped down from the stool to get the bananas.

"How about you mix the pudding, and I cut the

fruit, and then we can both place the vanilla wafers?"

She high-fived Mercy and took a seat at the table. It was beautiful to see the once quiet little girl come out of her shell.

Every once in a while, she talked about her mom, and it broke Mercy's heart to hear the stories about Maddie trying to wake her or when a nice lady came and took her to a sleepover. The only thing Mercy could figure was social services had picked her up.

"Are you happy, Maddie?"

"Yes."

Mercy gathered the ingredients and sat down beside her little helper.

"I'm glad." As a child, she spent hours in the kitchen cooking and baking with her mom. During those times, she learned the greatest lessons of her life, like patience, and that failure was okay, and although differences of opinions were tough, that's what makes us individuals.

She poured the milk into the pudding mix. If her mother knew she used instant, she'd be disowned.

"If we hurry, this will be ready by the time your daddy comes to get you."

"Is it a surprise?"

"Sure." Mercy ruffled her hair. "Surprises are nice."

On reflection, Alex was a pleasant surprise. He was a reasonable man or at least seemed to be. How funny that she'd completely disregarded him as a love interest. It's been said that opposites attract, and Alex was north to her south. He was famous, and she was forgettable, and yet, they seemed to have a connection beyond simple attraction. Somehow she was tethered to him by something deeper. Was it their twin desires to make sure Maddie's life was stable? She came from a place of love and wanting every child to have what she did. He came from a darker place where he wanted to make sure Maddie didn't have the childhood he had. He wanted better for her, and she respected that.

While they assembled the layers, Mercy considered her life, and just as she came to terms with falling in love with him, a soft knock sounded at the door.

"He's here, Maddie."

The light in her little eyes brightened. People said that a daughter's first crush was on her father, and Maddie was utterly smitten, but she couldn't blame her because Alex had a way of wheedling his way inside and settling in for the long haul.

She opened the door and found him holding a bag. "I brought burgers."

"Daddy!" Maddie wrapped her arms around his leg.

"Chicken fingers for you, young lady."

He looked up at Mercy and smiled, but there was something behind that smile that didn't feel quite right. She'd spent enough time with Alex to know when his expressions weren't his actual intent.

"Looks like we need to talk about something," she said.

He walked inside, dragging his leg with Maddie attached. "How did you know?"

Her stomach knotted. Anytime someone needed to talk, it wasn't good. "It's in your eyes. Your smile is radiant, but your eyes are dull."

He shook his head. "I don't know how your former husband got away with all he did."

"I wasn't as observant back then. I'm much more vigilant these days."

"Lucky me."

She assumed he was being sarcastic. "Is it something bad?" She had enough bad to last a lifetime.

"Not for me."

Her swallow was like shards of brittle glass slicing her throat. "But bad for me?" This was it; this was where he would tell her it was fun, but over.

"Let's eat, and then we'll talk."

She nodded, even though her stomach wouldn't be able to take food. He brought dinner, and she had to appreciate his thoughtfulness and Maddie's need to eat.

"Hey, Mads, let's set the table."

She let go of her father's leg and moved like an excited puppy to the kitchen.

Mercy took a step to follow.

"Hey," Alex said, reaching out to stop her. "It's not a bad thing, and it's not anything negative about us. I know your past experiences rule your present expectations. I'm not with anyone but you, and I don't want to be because you make me feel things I've never experienced before."

He lowered his lips to hers, and with a slow sensual kiss, he obliterated the fear and the fortress erected around her heart.

At the table, they enjoyed their meal with Mercy picking at her burger and Maddie using enough ketchup to meet her vitamin C requirements for the day.

Once done, Maddie went out back to play, and Mercy got a glass of wine because something told her she'd need it.

"Would you like one?" She raised the bottle of pinot grigio and lifted her chin.

"Sure."

Her heart stuttered because Alex never drank, and if this was a drinking moment, it was big.

She filled the glasses and led him to the patio table.

After a long drink, she straightened her shoulders. "Okay, spill."

Alex studied her for a few seconds, then sipped his wine. "I told you who my father was and what he did. He was an amazing guitarist and a member of one of the biggest bands of their time. The band got nominated for the Rock Music Hall of Fame."

"That's great."

"Yes, it is. While my father couldn't care less about awards, I think he'd find it funny that he had to wait until he was dead to get one." He shook his head. "Anyway, Pablo, the bass player, tracked me down and asked if I'd play at the ceremony."

Her heart swelled for him because music was important, and being there to watch his father get recognized for his contribution had to be validating to Alex.

"That's great. So, when do you leave?"

He gnawed at his lower lip. "So that's the thing. Although you renegotiated your pay, I need more from you, so we'll stick with the old rate. Besides, hasn't anyone told you not to negotiate down if you want to get ahead?"

"Although the money is nice, I refuse to be unfair."

"I'm asking for something big."

If leaving for a few days to honor his father is all he wanted, it was easy to give.

"I'll be happy to take care of Maddie. Just explain

to her that you'll be back in a few days."

He brought his glass to his lips and paused. "Here's the thing. The ceremony kicks off a tour, and I told them I'd do that too."

"You what?" She held back her anger and kept her voice at an even keel.

"I said I'd do it."

"Because you assumed I'd watch Maddie, and of course I will, but shouldn't you have checked first?" She pushed her chair back to gain distance. "Oh, that's right. I don't have much of a life, so there was no risk of me being busy."

He reached for her hand, but she kept it out of reach. This wasn't a time to get lost in his touch.

"You have a daughter who needs you."

"It's a bucket list item. You of all people should understand that."

"I get it, but there are times you need to set your needs aside to make sure others come first. I thought you didn't want to be like your father?"

He crossed his arms over his chest. "I'm not like my father."

"No? I didn't know him, but from what I've heard, he would have chosen his career over you any day. I thought you wanted better for your daughter."

"She's not my daughter." He rubbed the scruff on his face. "I got the results back a while ago."

She stared at him. "Why didn't you tell me?"

"Because it didn't matter. I love Maddie, and I want to give her a better life. I'll be gone for about five weeks. How much can change?"

She stared at him for several seconds. "Are you kidding me? We've known each other for less time and look at what's changed in both of our lives." She turned to see Maddie chase a big orange butterfly. "Weeks ago, she had a mother who died and was thrust in front of a man she didn't know. How scary is that? She's had enough change, and leaving for such a long period will send the same message your father sent to you. You didn't matter."

"But she does matter."

Mercy lifted from her seat. "Prove it." She walked down the steps and into the yard.

"Hey, Maddie," she glanced over her shoulder to Alex, whose thin-lipped expression was all she needed to see. "Your dad is ready to go."

She marched up the steps and into the house to get Maddie's backpack.

Alex rushed toward her, setting his hands on her shoulders. "Can't we talk about this more?"

She shook her head. "What's the point? You need to do what you have to." She pushed the backpack against his stomach. "I'll need most of her clothes and some of her favorite toys."

"Are we going to get past this?"

Why did she give her heart to the wrong men?

CHAPTER TWENTY-ONE

It broke Alex's heart to see Maddie's tears when he told her he had to go.

"Why, Daddy?"

He folded her shirts and placed them in one of his suitcases because her little Disney Princess one was too small. "It's not forever, honey. It's just a few weeks, and then I'll be back."

"Promise?"

How in the world did his father leave him? Surely, Alex had the same forlorn expression each time his dad took off. The difference was Alex knew he would come back, and since they weren't touring for another year, he'd stay.

"You get to stay with Mercy." Thoughts of her

twisted his gut. The look of disappointment on her face hollowed him out.

Part of him understood his father's aversion to attachments. By marrying Alex's mother and offering financial support, he fulfilled what he believed were his obligations.

"How about we call Mercy and ask her to meet us for breakfast?" He closed the suitcase and picked Maddie up. "You can have those chocolate chip pancakes you love."

He held her tightly. The thought of letting her go was painful, but he knew if he didn't do the gig, he'd always regret it.

Maddie wrapped her little arms around his neck. "I love Mercy, and I love you."

"I love you both too." He'd never been in love. All these years, he let another organ rule his life, but this feeling he had deep in his soul was different. Her disappointment in him mattered. He wanted to be more for her too.

He took his phone from his pocket and dialed Mercy.

"Hey," she answered. She always had this breathy thing to her voice that heated him from the inside out.

"Good morning." He shifted to put Maddie higher on his hip. "I know you're mad at me, but I hoped you'd meet us for breakfast at Maisey's."

There was a pause. "I'm not mad at you. I get why you're doing it, but I'm disappointed in your choices."

He walked to the living room and swiped his keys from the table. "I bet you bring your students to tears."

"Only if they're guilty."

"Should I come to get you?" He was already out the door.

"I'll meet you there. When?"

"Now, I miss you, and I'll make it up to you."

"Make it up to Maddie."

He buckled his girl into her booster seat, and they headed to Maisey's, where he let Maddie pick the table. She seemed to like the one in the back corner. They sat there and waited a few minutes for Mercy.

She took his breath away when she entered. Her hair fell in waves around her shoulders. Those jeans she wore were the kind a man could get jealous of with how they hugged her figure.

A smile softened her features, but he saw underlying questions in her eyes.

When he rose and softly kissed her, she hesitated before returning his affection.

"Thank you for the invite." Rather than sit next to him, she took the space beside Maddie. "Hey, kiddo, how are you?"

Maddie shrugged her shoulders. "I'm sad because Daddy is leaving."

Mercy pulled Maddie to her side. "He'll be back. And who knows, maybe we can watch the award ceremony on TV, so you don't miss him too much." She lifted her eyes to meet his. "Do you have anything else you need me to do? I mean, you're paying for far more than what you're getting."

"You are mad at me."

She shook her head. "No, I'm conflicted. I thought you were different, but you're exactly who I thought you were the first time I met you, and I'm mad at myself for falling so fast."

"What does that mean?"

"It means that you're a musician first."

"It's only one part of who I am." Heat raced up his spine. "I'm more than that."

"You're right, and I'm being unfair. I do get it because I also had a bucket list. On the one hand, I'm glad you can fulfill a dream, but this won't be easy on Maddie."

She pulled a coloring book out of her purse and placed it in front of Maddie. "You want to color, sweetheart?" Mercy was like Mary Poppins with a bag that had everything anyone needed.

Maisey sauntered over. "What's it going to be, kids?"

"Pancakes with chocolate chips for the princess, and I'll have a waffle and bacon," Mercy said.

Maisey turned her attention to Alex. "I don't

think I have mentioned this, but I like that new haircut. I bet you get a lot more attention now that people can see your eyes."

Like a woman army crawling across my lawn this morning kind of attention

"Oh, I haven't really noticed because I'm only interested in one woman." He laid his hand on top of Mercy's.

Maisey sighed. "Young love."

"It's not that serious," Mercy said.

"The hell it's not." He squeezed her hand.

"Looks like you have some talking to do." Maisey glanced at Maddie and then at him. "What are you hankering for?"

"Peace and patience, but I'll settle for pancakes and sausage."

"You got it." She started to turn and then stopped. "Can Maddie come back to the kitchen with me? Ben could use an assistant. She'll be safe."

He looked to Mercy for an answer while she stared at him. It was Maddie who made the decision. "Can I make the pancakes?" She slithered under the table and popped out the other side. "With a smiley face?"

"That's the only kind." Maisey lifted her chin at Alex. "Okay with you, Dad?"

"Yes, but I want extra love in mine."

As soon as they left, he turned his attention back

to Mercy. "This doesn't change the way I feel about you."

"I care about you too, and that's what worries me."

"I'm not a cheater."

"How do you know? You've never had a long-term relationship."

He let her hand go. "Maybe not, but I've also never had a girl I wanted to turn into long-term until I met you. If this is going to work, you have to trust me."

She drew in a deep breath. "If this is going to work, you need to earn my trust."

"I don't like your husband."

"Deceased husband, and you could never despise him as much as I do."

He got up and moved next to her. "I hate that he took your trust before I could ever earn it."

Moments later, Maddie and Maisey were back with breakfast. And as they ate, he looked at what he'd started to believe was his family. Doc was right; DNA didn't make a daddy.

ALEX SAT in his first-class chair and thought about the last two days. Mercy was reserved but loving. They never got the alone time he craved. Time to prove to her that she was his, but they spent family time together with Maddie.

Heartbreaking is when your child cries because you're walking away. A significant part of him battled with getting on the plane, but he made a commitment and would honor it. Even that ate at him because he made a bigger commitment to Maddie and failed her.

The flight crew made their announcements, and in minutes, the plane was in the air. There was no turning back now. He opened his carry-on to grab the music Pablo emailed and found Maddie's bear. This was no accident. She'd put it there for him. Was it so he'd remember her, or was it to protect him? He smiled, brought it to his nose, and inhaled her scent. She always smelled like lavender, just like Mercy—Mommy Mercy. She would make a great mom—did make one for Maddie. While he was gone, he had some thinking to do about his life. Where it was and where he wanted it to be.

CHAPTER TWENTY-TWO

Mercy woke up with a ball of heat tucked next to her and stroked Maddie's hair away from her face. It had been three days since Alex left, and they were the longest of her life. Somewhere between he's not her type and his flight to Los Angeles, she fell in love with him.

It didn't work in her favor that Maddie had pulled every other heartstring she had.

Maddie's sleepy eyes fluttered open, and she stared into Mercy's. This was supposed to be her life —beautiful daughter, faithful husband, satisfying job. People say you can't have it all, but why not?

She kissed the top of Maddie's head. "Are you hungry?"

She snuggled closer to Mercy. "Five more minutes."

Mercy laughed. "We can cuddle all day if you like."

"Where's Daddy?" She asked the same question about ten times a day.

"He's in Los Angeles. We get to see him on television tonight."

"I am so excited."

"Me too, sweetheart."

Alex deserved some credit; he called several times a day and sent flowers to both of them. Maddie's were the bright-colored daisies, and hers were red roses. If she dug deep into the meaning, those indicated love, but would a man who loved her leave?

She was being ridiculous and knew it. This was on his bucket list, and dreams should be realized, or at least chased. Who could fault him for wanting to play in his dad's band?

It was more than playing at the awards ceremony for Alex. This was all about the validation his father never gave him. To step on stage and into his father's shoes meant that he'd made it. He had craved his dad's approval and never got it, so this gig was a way of putting that to rest. If Alex Cruz was good enough to play his father's music, he must be good enough.

"How about we get a bowl of cereal and veg out on the couch with cartoons or a Disney movie?"

Maddie was halfway off the bed. "Little Mermaid." She ran barefooted to the living room.

Mercy was certain by the time she got there, Maddie would already have the television tuned to the Disney Channel, a gift from Alex before he left.

"Cheerios or Apple Jacks?" she asked.

"Cheerios," Maddie answered.

A few minutes later, they cuddled beside each other and watched Princess Ariel find her happily ever after.

At two o'clock, Alex called. He had his own ringtone that Maddie picked out. It was barking dogs, and when Mercy asked why, all she said was she liked dogs and her daddy.

Kids were simple. There was no deception; they were who they were.

"Do you want to answer?" She handed her phone to Maddie, who squealed an excited hello.

For the next ten minutes, she watched her grow more animated, telling Alex about Ariel and Prince Eric and how someday she would marry a prince, and they could all live in the castle together.

"Daddy wants to talk to you."

Why did her heart flutter every time? She was supposed to be mad at him but who didn't love a bad boy who turned out to be a good man. He'd accepted responsibility for a child that wasn't even his because he wanted her to have a better life. How could she not love him for that?

"Hey, you. Are you nervous?"

Though he'd never admit it, she thought he probably was. This wasn't a crowd of fifty thousand, it was millions across the globe tuning into the show.

"Nervous? Not about the show."

What else would he be nervous about? "Do you need to talk about it?"

"I'm just working some stuff out in my head. You gave me a lot to think about when you told me I needed to prove it."

A pang of guilt pricked her heart. "I may have been too hard on you."

"No, I don't think you were. One thing is for sure, and that's I need you."

"You need me?" That was a stretch for a man who could have anyone, but she liked how it sounded.

"I do. You're wise and kind, and your priorities are straight."

She laughed. "My priorities have to be, or I'm homeless."

"I'd never let that happen to you." There was a pause. "I miss you, Mercy. More than I ever thought possible, and I'm so sorry I disappointed you."

"I'm sorry too. We're learning all this together. Children are my specialty—"

"Bet you didn't expect to have a thirty-eight-year-old kid on your hands."

"That wasn't even a thought in my mind. I was going to say that children are easy, but this adulting stuff is tougher than it looks. I miss you too. When you get back, can we start over again?" She held her breath, waiting for his reply.

"No."

Her heart tumbled to her gut. "No?"

"I don't want to start over; I want to continue. We took a detour, but that doesn't mean I want to start at the beginning. I like where we are."

"You in California and me in Colorado?"

"No. Together where it matters, where our hearts collide."

"You should write that down. It sounds like a love song."

"Do you want me to write you a love song?"

Her heart rose from the pit of her stomach to dance in her chest.

"No one ever has."

"Then I'll write you a love song."

She couldn't help the roll of her eyes that he would never see. "Shouldn't you be in love with me before you write me a song?"

"Who says I'm not?" His name was called in the background. "I've got to go, but if you're watching tonight, I'll blow you a kiss."

"I'll be watching."

When they hung up, she stared at the TV and saw nothing. His words kept moving through her head in slow motion. *Who says I'm not?*

She picked up her phone and dialed her mom.

"Hello, Mimi, how's my baby girl?"

"Mom, I think I'm in love."

In the background, she could hear the grinding of mom's kitchen chair against the tile. "With the drummer?"

Over the weeks, they had short conversations about Alex and Maddie, but she didn't divulge much because her mother coined the phrase, "enquiring minds want to know," and there were no boundaries when it came to her mom.

"Yes, the drummer, but he's more than that. He's a good man and an excellent father, despite not having a role model."

"More importantly, is he good in bed?" There was a crackling of paper and a hum from her mother.

"What are you eating?"

"Skinny Pop, this is going to be good, and I needed a snack."

"I'm not divulging details." She wasn't going to give her mom the blow by blow. "But I'll say it's amazing." It truly was. She never had her body sing for a man, but Alex knew how to pluck the right strings, hit the right notes, and bang out a perfect rhythm.

"Come on, Mimi; it's girl talk."

The crunch of popcorn filled her ear.

"Let's just say that I've never ever felt like I do when I'm with him."

Mom laughed. "Take a picture of my grandbaby and tell her Grandma already loves her."

"Aren't you moving a little fast?"

"I don't think so. Things tend to move faster when there are two things to love. Hell, if you got a puppy before he left, you'd hit the trifecta."

"What about the groupies? I have to trust him, but it's hard."

"He doesn't need to be on tour to have a love affair. They can happen from the safety of your couch."

Mom was right. There was always someone willing and waiting. "I know. I've got to trust."

"It's okay to be cautious with your heart; just don't make him accountable for another man's sins."

"It is hard not to because Randy blindsided me. But I am learning that not all men are like him. Alex is one of the good ones, and I think he loves me."

"Oh, honey, how could he not?" More crunching. "What time did you say that the awards show was on?"

"I didn't, but it's at seven."

"Gotta stalk my future son-in-law. Maybe he can teach your dad to play the drums. As we age, we lose some of that dexterity, or maybe he's gotten lazy."

"Dad? Lazy? I doubt it." Her parents never lost their appetite for each other. That's what she wanted.

CHAPTER TWENTY-THREE

Alex stood on the stage, looking at the crowd and listening to the roar of adoring fans. All the while, he wished he was in Aspen Cove with Mercy and Maddie.

"You ready for this?" Pablo asked.

"I'm set." He'd been ready his whole life. It's what he thought he wanted—the love and adoration of fans and respect of his father, but now that he was here, it felt hollow as if somehow he chased the wrong dream.

A glance at Maddie's teddy bear, which he set on the amplifier, made his heart ache for his little family. That's exactly what they were, his family.

Pablo counted off the song, and the drummer set

the pace. It was surreal to stand on the stage where his father had played so many times.

In his hand was Dad's favorite guitar that Alex rarely played because it seemed sacred. But it wasn't. For far too long, he'd worshipped the wrong things; he knew that now.

The band played three of their biggest hits, and just before he left the stage, he blew a kiss at the camera and hoped his girls got it. He swiped Maddie's bear and headed toward the greenroom.

Backstage were the groupies, with their plumped lips and bouncing breasts. How was it that he'd been content with so little?

"Hey, Axel?" A blonde sidled up to him, calling his stage name. "You're on my bucket list."

He hugged the bear closer to his chest, turned, and smiled at the woman. "Can I give you some advice?"

She reached out to touch his shirt, and he jumped back.

"I'll do anything you tell me," she purred.

"Good, because this is important." He studied her for a moment. "Update your bucket list. Put things on it that will lift you up instead of tear you down. Being someone's one-night stand won't ever be the end all and be all. When you're older and wondering what the hell happened to your life, you don't want groupie trophies lining your memory shelf. You owe it to yourself to be better."

He turned and walked away, and a second later, she called out, "Hey, Pablo, you're on my bucket list."

"Hold that thought, sweetheart," Pablo rushed to Alex. "We've got a few days, and then it's tour time." He looked over his shoulder to the blonde. "I'll share."

Alex shook his head. "Not my type."

Pablo's eyes grew wide. "You got a type?"

He closed his eyes and pictured Mercy. "Yep, a sweet schoolteacher with motherly instincts."

"Is that some new kind of fetish, like a hot librarian?"

Alex chuckled. "Nah, man, that's love." He moved down the hall and entered the room where he'd stored his things. Everything he brought, save for the guitar and the bear, was at the hotel. He set the guitar against the wall, tucked the bear under his arm, and walked to the door. He had no problem traveling light when his heart was so full.

He passed the roadie on the way out. "There's a guitar in the greenroom. It's yours, man."

"What? Are you serious? Why would you do that?"

"I don't need to hold on to the past any longer. I'm racing for my future."

He walked outside the venue and climbed into a waiting cab.

"Where to?"

"Airport, please."

CHAPTER TWENTY-FOUR

Mercy laughed. "Honey, it doesn't matter how many times you change the channel, your father is not on the television anymore."

"I miss Daddy."

She tugged Maddie to her and held tightly. "I miss him too, but he called and said hello, and that's all we have for right now." She looked down at the little girl in her arms. This was the way life was supposed to be—almost. To make it perfect would take Alex there, hugging them both.

"Let's pack lunch, and we'll go to the park early and get a place close to the stage."

"And see Daddy?"

Typical five-year-old. Maddie was like a dog with

a bone when she got something into her head, and right now, all she wanted was her father.

"Wouldn't that be nice?" It was better to answer with an open-ended question than have to explain that Alex was on a vision quest. "Peanut butter and jelly or turkey?"

Maddie strutted to the pantry and took out the peanut butter jar. "Grape jelly, please."

BY THE TIME THEY ARRIVED, the crowd was building, and the Aspen Cove firefighters walked around handing out plastic hats and filling empty boots with donations. Before Samantha came to town, this would have been an ordinary August day, but it carried the popularity of a county fair, bringing people from all over.

A part of her was glad Alex wasn't here. There were so many beautiful women hanging out for a chance to hook up. She wanted to march up to them and say, "Show yourself some respect," but she didn't. Even her mother had been a groupie once.

"Daddy's here." Maddie bolted from the blanket, but Mercy had lightning reflexes and caught the hem of her shirt, tugging her back.

"He's in Los Angeles, sweetie."

"No, he's here."

Mercy patted the blanket next to her. "Come sit with me. The band is about to play."

Samantha walked out, and the crowd erupted into applause.

"Hello," she shouted and waved. "Welcome to our annual Fireman's Fundraiser, which became a thing when my house burned down. The town of Aspen Cove had a wonderful volunteer fire department, and the people who came to my rescue did so without reservation. In return, I hold this concert every year to fund the new fire department as my way of giving back. Are you ready to party?"

The roar of the crowd was deafening. Samantha tapped on the mic to get their attention.

"Before we begin, I want to introduce the band." She pointed to her right. "On the bass is Gray Stratton." Then she turned to her left. "On the guitar is Red Blakely. Today we also have a guest filling in. Originally, he was taking Alex Cruz's place, but Alex is here." The women went wild.

Mercy stood up so she could see the drummer who was obstructed by the cymbals.

"Turns out he loves Aspen Cove and couldn't stay away, or maybe it's something else like a hazel-eyed little girl and a pretty schoolteacher. Anyway, Axel or Alex, as we know him, is on the drums. That leaves Griffin Taylor, who is hanging out with the band today. He's a musical sorcerer and can play anything, so he's taking over the keyboards. Maybe we can convince him to stay."

Mercy craned to see Alex.

"Told you," Maddie said.

"Yes, you did."

A tap on her shoulder drew her attention from the stage.

Dalton stood beside her. "I've set up some seats for you and Maddie. Alex wants you to come up on stage with him."

"He does?"

He nodded. "That's where family belongs." He helped her gather her things while the band played their first song.

Dalton slid headphones over Maddie's ears before she took the steps to the stage.

Sweat dripped from Alex's face as he played, and when he saw her approach, his smile broadened. He never looked so happy.

And as soon as the song finished, he stood and held his arms out to Maddie, and she flung herself into his embrace.

"Oh, Daddy, I missed you."

"Missed you too, squirt."

Mercy's heart nearly exploded seeing them together. Family was what you created, and a perfect one stood before her.

Alex slid Maddie to her feet and locked eyes with Mercy.

"Why are you standing there and not here next to me?" He crooked a finger and called her over.

She looked at the band, who waited for Alex to take his seat at the drums. "You've got a concert to perform."

"I do, but my priorities are straight now, and I've got a woman to kiss." His words echoed over the loudspeaker. "Get over here and kiss me, Mercy. I can't live another minute without a taste of you on my lips."

There was a collective sigh from the audience.

Mercy moved toward Alex. She didn't have a demonstrative personality. She preferred the sidelines to the limelight but couldn't pass up an opportunity to kiss him.

Like Maddie, she flung herself into his open arms. When his mouth covered hers, the world silenced, and only his taste, scent, and love existed. She was in Alex's arms and wanted to stay there.

He ended the kiss much too quickly. "Stay right there because I've got a surprise for you." He kissed her again before he moved back to his drums.

She stayed nearby with Maddie in front of her while they watched and listened.

A thousand hearts broke the moment he kissed her. In front of God and the world, Alex told everyone he loved her. Each song they played, he stared at her with such adoration that she understood what it was that drew every woman to him. It wasn't his looks, even though he was hotter than Hades. He had a smile that could disintegrate the panties off a woman, but that's not what drew her in. It was his heart. It wasn't always easy to do the right thing at the right time, and yet, here he was.

As the concert came to an end, Alex left the drums. He wrapped one arm around her and the other around Maddie and led them to the front of the stage.

Samantha smiled at him and handed over her guitar. Red rushed forward with a chair that Mercy thought Alex would take, but he didn't. Alex led her to it and lifted Maddie into her lap before turning to the crowd.

"I'd like to introduce the two most important women in my life. They both arrived unexpectedly, as most surprises do." He ruffled the hair on Maddie's head. "This is my daughter, Maddie. She's a brilliant and beautiful young lady." He took in a big breath. "I thought I was the one that could offer her everything, but I was wrong. She came into my life and brought the sun with her, and nothing lives without that. She gives me more than I could ever return." He settled the guitar over his neck and adjusted the strap. "The beautiful woman with my daughter is Mercy, and Lord have mercy on my heart when it comes to her." He kissed her forehead and dropped to his knees. "She once told me she wanted a love song, so here it is."

He plucked the notes on the guitar and strummed a soft ballad.

His voice was whiskey smooth and velvety soft, and she stared into his eyes while he sang her a love song.

There is no love without you.

You're the something I never knew I needed. Like a warm embrace or a smile across your face.

You're the sigh at the end of a breath. I want to give you my all until there's nothing left.

You belong with me. Let's live together side by side in the place where our hearts collide.

I have no use for love unless it comes from you.

When he finished, he waited, but she couldn't see him through her tears.

She swiped at the joy spilling from her eyes.

"You wrote that for me?"

He handed the guitar back to Samantha, who nodded toward Griffin. "Let's finish this with one of my favorites. It's called 'Lucky,' and I wrote it when I met my husband, Dalton." She glanced at Mercy, Maddie, and Alex. "Looks like someone else is getting lucky."

"That's your hint to leave," Dalton said. "Get out of here before the crowd dissipates."

Alex picked up Maddie and led Mercy down the steps. They wove through the crowd, not stopping once until they got to his SUV, and as soon as they were all safely inside, he turned to her.

"I'm so sorry."

She couldn't imagine what for. "Don't you dare take back that love song."

He drove off and placed his hand over hers. "Not in a million years. I love you, Mercy, and I'm going to write you a million more songs."

"What about me, Daddy, will you write me a song too?"

"You bet, squirt."

"Why didn't you tell us you were coming home for the concert?"

He squeezed her hand. "I didn't come for the concert. I came home for you and Maddie. It's incredibly hard to live without my heart."

"Where are we going?"

"Home."

"Whose home?"

He pulled her hand to his lips, nearly pulling her over the center console. "Mercy, wherever you are is home to me. You tell me where you want to go."

"There's food at my house."

He turned down Daisy Lane. "Are you trying to speak to my baser needs?"

She giggled. Who knew that a schoolteacher from Aspen Cove could speak to any of his needs? "If we're going straight to your baser requirements, I'm not sure food will fill those."

He let out a little growl. "You're right." He parked the car and helped them out. With Maddie in his arms, he led them up the walkway. "Hey, Mads, let's play for a while, and after that, would you like to have a sleepover at Ms. Louise's?"

Maddie danced around him. "Can I bring my Barbie?"

"Anything you want."

THREE HOURS LATER, they were alone.

"When does the tour start?"

He chuckled. "Right now." He swept her into his arms and carried her to her bed.

After slowly stripping off her clothes, he started at her feet and worked his way up her body, spending long minutes playing her like one of his instruments, and oh, how he made her sing.

Several hums left her lips.

"Yep, you're in tune," he said.

"Oh, I don't know, don't you think you should recheck?"

"You're right. I'll reconfirm all night long."

The second time they made love, she lay with her head on his shoulder and her hand over his heart. Mercy had never been so satisfied in all her life, but something was still niggling in the back of her mind.

"So, you're not going back to play with the band?"

He shook his head. "No, I don't need the band. The only thing I get from going on tour is a paycheck, and I'm pretty pat when it comes to money. I thought I needed the validation, but all I need is you and Maddie."

"How did this happen?"

He kissed the top of her head. "You tried to be a groupie."

Once Maddie drew her family on the back of the list, Mercy no longer thought about what she wanted. She didn't need to be a groupie when she had her own rock star. Didn't need to wish for a child when she had Maddie. Earth-shattering Os were a given anytime she and Alex found the time to pleasure one another.

"I'm the last groupie you'll ever have."

He kissed her long, hard, and passionately. "You're the only groupie I want."

CHAPTER TWENTY-FIVE

Several weeks later.

Alex walked through his home, and it was different. Not because of the art on the walls, or the touches of light and life Mercy infused with her throw pillows and knickknacks. No, it was different because love lived here.

"Are you almost ready?" he called to Maddie.

She burst out of her room, wearing a pretty pink dress and stood beside him. Mercy was due home soon from setting up her classroom. While she didn't spend the night with him and Maddie regularly, they made his house their home base for all family activities.

The nights were the hardest to bear, but after tonight, he hoped they could consolidate. He didn't care if they moved to her house or she moved to his. All he wanted was to get his family in one place.

Her crazy Volkswagen bug pulled into the driveway.

"She's here, Mads. Get the flowers."

He'd been as calm as a tranquil sea until a minute ago. What was about to go down would either be the biggest accomplishment of his life or the greatest disappointment. He checked his pocket and waited for her to walk inside.

The door swung open, and Mercy entered.

"Hey, guys." It took her a second to realize that Maddie was in a dress, and he was in a suit. "Is there something I should know about?"

Maddie ran to her and handed her the flowers. "Yes, Daddy wants to know if you'll marry us."

He couldn't hold the laugh back. "Honey, that was my part." He studied Mercy to see what she might be thinking, and all he saw was love in her eyes.

"Is this—"

"Come here, beautiful." He held out his hand and walked her to the couch, where he helped her take a seat. On one knee in front of her, he said, "Mercy Meyer, nothing in my life has been the same since I met you. The thing is, up until then, I thought my life had everything. But you taught me that it was nothing without love, and it is nothing, without you."

He pulled the box from his pocket; it wasn't a huge diamond, but it was a perfect diamond to reflect how perfect she was to him. "Will you marry me?"

"And me," Maddie said.

"Isn't this too soon?"

That was an argument he expected. "You're right, it is soon, but that doesn't mean it's wrong. What do you say, take a chance on me?"

She lifted her chin. "Will you write me more love songs?"

"Absolutely."

"What about the fence outside? I never once dreamed of a house with a chain-link fence."

"I'll get Wes on the pickets tomorrow."

"I want to plant things."

He bit his lip and quirked a brow. "Me too, Maddy wants a brother."

"Can we name him Strawberry Sam?" Maddie asked.

"Not if you want him safe at school," Mercy said. She turned to face Alex. "You want to marry me, have more children, and put up a white picket fence?"

He opened the box and removed the diamond. "I want to love you, and the rest we'll figure out along the way." He grinned. "However, I'm totally up for the planting as soon as you are."

A tear slipped down her cheek. "Yes. I'll marry you both."

He slipped the ring on her finger, and for the first time in his life, he felt whole.

He didn't need fame. He still liked having his fortune, but if it all went away, as long as he had Mercy and Maddie, he'd be happy.

CHAPTER TWENTY-SIX

Mercy rushed out of Doc's office with a smile on her face. She had to give it to Alex. When he put his mind to something, he was all in. A week after he put that ring on her finger, he asked Doc to marry them. They stood at the end of Katie and Bowie's dock and said their vows.

The picket fence was up, and the backyard was tilled for next year's garden. She said goodbye to her little place on Daisy Lane and moved in with her family.

She glanced down at the test results in her hand. Pregnant.

Months ago, her life was hard, but hard didn't turn out to be hollow or hellish or any other negative

H in the alphabet; it turned out to be heavenly, happy, and hopeful.

She loved her new life, but Alex didn't have a clue just how much was about to change, but she entered the corner store hoping to find a way to drop the hint. Maybe a package of diapers or a baby bottle on the table would be perfect.

Instead, she found Deanna and Red in an argument, and the new owner, Jewel, sitting behind the counter, taking it all in.

Jewel nodded. "What you're looking for is in aisle three."

Mercy cocked her head to the side. "What?"

"Just trust me."

Mercy moved down to the third aisle and turned the corner, running straight into Alex.

"What are you doing here?"

He smiled. "Taking care of my family. Are you ready to tell me?"

The heat of a blush rushed to her cheeks. "How did you know?"

He held up a box of saltines and a bottle of Sprite. "Did you think I didn't notice these laying around the house?"

Toward the front of the store next to a Hostess display, Deanna yelled, "I wouldn't sleep with you again even if you were the last man on earth."

Red snapped back. "This is Aspen Cove, baby,

and I am the last man unless you're into Peter Larkin."

Mercy and Alex peeked around the corner to watch the drama unfold.

Jewel laughed. "Almost better than TV."

Deputy Sheriff Merrick walked through the door and caught Red and Deanna arguing.

"Everything okay here?"

Deanna walked up to Merrick and pulled him down for a kiss.

"What the hell are you doing?" Red yelled.

Deanna stepped back and looked at Merrick. "Everything you won't, as long as he's willing." She patted his chest. "Hey, Merrick, I've got a pizza and a six-pack of beer if you're game."

Merrick looked between the two. "I like pizza."

"Great, six o'clock at my house. I live on Daisy Lane." She looked at Mercy and Alex. "Be careful, though, it's a lucky for love street."

"I like love," Merrick answered.

Red crossed his arms. "What are you doing, Deanna?"

"I'm moving on, Red. I want someone to love me."

Mercy looked at Deanna, and her heart ached. It wasn't that long ago she had felt the same way, but she wasn't sure if it would happen. Then she met Alex, who taught her to open up, trust, and so many other lessons on love. As she gazed into her husband's eyes and recited the first line of the love song he wrote her, "There is no love without you," she realized no truer words were ever spoken.

Next up is One Hundred Mistakes

OTHER BOOKS BY KELLY COLLINS

Recipes for Love

A Tablespoon of Temptation

A Pinch of Passion

A Dash of Desire

A Cup of Compassion

A Dollop of Delight

A Layer of Love

Recipe for Love Collection 1-3

The Second Chance Series

Set Free

Set Aside

Set in Stone

Set Up

Set on You

The Second Chance Series Box Set

A Pure Decadence Series

Yours to Have

Yours to Conquer

Yours to Protect

A Pure Decadence Collection

Wilde Love Series

Betting On Him

Betting On Her

Betting On Us

A Wilde Love Collection

The Boys of Fury Series

Redeeming Ryker

Saving Silas

Delivering Decker

The Boys of Fury Boxset

Making the Grade Series

The Dean's List

Honor Roll

The Learning Curve

Making the Grade Box Set

Stand Alone Billionaire Novels

Dream Maker

GET A FREE BOOK.

Go to www.authorkellycollins.com

ABOUT THE AUTHOR

International bestselling author of more than thirty novels, Kelly Collins writes with the intention of keeping love alive. Always a romantic, she blends real-life events with her vivid imagination to create characters and stories that lovers of contemporary romance, new adult, and romantic suspense will return to again and again.

Kelly lives in Colorado at the base of the Rocky Mountains with her husband of twenty-seven years, their two dogs, and a bird that hates her. She has three amazing children, whom she loves to pieces.

For More Information
www.authorkellycollins.com
kelly@authorkellycollins.com